Tanrı Dedi Işık Olsun

JN097068

Stean Anthony

Yamaguchi Shoten, Kyoto

山口書店, 京都

Title of book: Tanrı dedi, "Işık olsun."

Turkish Gen 1.3 "God said, Let there be light."

I follow this biblical translation for Turkish:

Elohim [Gen 1.1] = Theos = Deus = God = Tanrı

Hashem [Tetragrammaton] = Kyrios = Dominus = LORD = Allah

Image on the cover of this book:

While conducting a census of nearly 100 galaxies in the nearby Universe, the PHANGS survey observed NGC0628, a galaxy with pure grand-design spiral morphology. NGC0628 is shown here as an ALMA (orange) composite with Hubble Space Telescope (red) data.

Credit: ALMA (ESO/NAOJ/NRAO)/ESA/NASA/PHANGS, S. Dagnello (NRAO)

Website: https://public.nrao.edu/gallery/phangs-alma-2/

TANRI DEDI IŞIK OLSUN

Author's profits

See end of book for details

PRINTED IN JAPAN

IN LOVE AND PEACE
FOR TURKS & GREEKS

Tanrı Dedi Işık Olsun

Contents

Episode Number & Title

6

8

12

367. Topkapı Hammam
368. Baghdad Kiosk
369. Lale Osman Tulip
370. Hagia Eirene Sacred Peace
371. Islamic Art
372. Sajjadah Carpet
373. Hippodrome
374. Avrasya Tunnel
375. Maiden's Tower
376. Kuzguncuk Bostanı
377. Basilica Cistern
378. Slender Tower
379. Ottoman Princess
380. Aya Sofiya Mosque
381. Square the Circle
382. Byzantine Diadem
383. Ivory Angel
384. Galleries
385. Marbles
386. Young Man
387. Seraphim
388. Theotokos Apse
389. Deësis
390. Hagia Sophia
391. Madman
392. Slow Bowler
393. Bad

18

Acknowledgements

Episodes with information about Sufism indebted to books by Kabir Helminski
   and others (Ep. 169 ff).
The Rumi Collection: An Anthology of Translations of Mevlana Jalaluddin Rumi.
   Sel. & ed. Kabir Helminski. Boston: Shambhala, 2005.
Love's Ripening: Rumi on the Heart's Journey. Trans. by Kabir Helminski &
   Ahmad Rezwami. Boston: Shambhala, 2008.
"The Threshold Society" is good: https://sufism.org/
Many episodes owe a debt to *Rick Steves: Istanbul* by Lale Surmen Aran &
   Tankut Aran. Eighth Edition. 2021.
Some episodes indebted to the Metropolitan Museum of New York.
Christian Classics Ethereal Library for Church Father texts.
   https://www.ccel.org/
Sunlight website has good translations of Rumi.
   http://sunlightgroup.blogspot.com/
Annemarie Schimmel, *Rumi's World.* Boston: Shambala, 2001. First ed. *I am*
   Wind, You are Fire. Boston: Shambhala, 1992.
Educational clips by Smarthistory with Khan Academy were helpful (YouTube).
Istanbul travel video by Bery Istanbul (YouTube) was helpful.
Istanbul information by Robin Pierson (YouTube) was helpful.

Information in this book comes from various sources. The story is fictional, and
the characters fictional. The purpose is educational, and the point of view is that
of the author alone and does not represent an official point of view of church or
institution.

Preface

This is a serialized novel, originally in the form of a calendar, now with numbered episodes. The central character is Phim, who appeared in *Exnihil* (Book 1), *Bərešitbara* (Book 2), *Enarchae* (Book 3), *Samāwātiwal'ard* (Book 4) and now *Tanrı Dedi Işık Olsun* (Book 5). Phim also appears in my earlier novel, *Mosaic Angel* (still unfinished). There is a paragraph of prose per day. Snapshots of story, poetic phrases.

1 Irma Crash-Landing

There was grim preparation going on rapidly by the ground staff. Plane coming in, possible crash landing. Get ready. 30 seconds counting 29, 28. Phim and the others were praying with all their might, holding hands together. Phim was hearing Irma singing, her voice so strong and brave. We're going to crash-land, she cried, Bless you Phim! Meanwhile, the Ottoman Mehter Band were playing "Well, hello Dolly," as the Turkish Airline 737 made a smooth one engine landing on the runway, to the assembled cheers of the public. Irma had arrived, and safely. Thank God, wept Phim, utterly overcome.

2 Abraham's Pool, Sanliurfa

Good to be together again, Phim, said Irma, briefly holding his hand. The Merc was speeding eastwards, crossing the Euphrates after Gaziantep. They parked in the centre of Sanliurfa. They walked in the garden containing the pool of Abraham, said to be where Abraham was saved from a vengeful Nimrod. A sacred cave nearby was his birthplace. Stone arches ran alongside the rectangular pool filled with carp. A mosque. A bride wearing white was reflected in the water. Holy fish, said Phim, throwing bread pellets. Poh! Poh! said the grey-green carp. That's teşekkür ederim in Carpish, laughed Yaeli.

(Teşekkür ederim: thank you in Turkish)

3   Ataturk Dam, Kahta

Sal pronounced, The river gave us life; the river lights our fires.   Phim said, A mighty achievement inconceivable to ancient peoples.   Joseph said, Maybe they'd have thought it wrong. Chaining up a river of Eden.   Yaeli said, The beauty of clean energy constantly available.   Sudan said, I feel terrible danger. We conquer the natural world. We do not give back. Look at the data. There were once forests along the Euphrates. Marshes. Abundant wildlife. So many extinct.   Look at this soft-shelled turtle.   Green Rafetus euphraticus peered from the iPhone. It's my Euphrates. The water tastes bad.

(Gen 2.10-14)

4   Deyrulzafaran Manastiri

The monastery was set on a slope above fields of olive trees. It was built with the same honey-colored limestone as Mardin. Joseph had asked to stay. They were given rooms. They would attend liturgy the following morning. It was a dawn service. Phim gazed on the Greek cross set in an exquisitely carved alcove which had imitation muqarnas above, and a cross within. It was a hybrid between a mihrab and an apse. Two lamps were burning. The Holy Bible in a silver cover. The priest opened the book and sang in Aramaic.

(Saffron Monastery near Mardin, Syrian Orthodox Church)

5   Shamash

The young priest explained. The monastery was built on the site of an ancient temple to the sun god, called Utu, worshipped by Babylonians as Shamash. He was the Mesopotamian sun god, a god of justice, morality, and truth, and the twin of the Mesopotamian goddess Inanna (also called Ishtar), who was the Queen of Heaven. He was a good god. He rode the heavens in his chariot. He was bearded and long-armed. His name survives in Hebrew. Obviously, he was a foreshadowing in ancient thinking of the true God of Israel, the creator of the sun and moon.

6   Mardin Donkey

They were walking in the backstreets. A donkey had been left standing by the wall. It was a paved street with stone walls. The donkey had panniers with a harness that ran tightly round his front. He was collecting the trash bags. He was white. A tourist scratched his head. How soft! Phim looked at him and thought, How many thousand years have we used you like this. The donkey said, without looking up, Don't repeat the bleeding obvious. Get me a carrot if you've got an ounce of compassion. He stood quietly ignoring them, staring at the wall.

7 Dicle Bridge, Diyarbakir

They parked the Merc and walked over the Tigris Bridge south of the city. It was a massive ancient bridge built of the same black basalt they used for the city walls. Mighty plinths with ten arches. No flood would carry me away. It flowed south, then east, and south again, eventually finding the sea; watering the beginnings of human civilization along the way. Phim and Sudan stood gazing on the water. It was a tranquil day. Blue sky and clouds moved through the calm surface. Phim wondered at it, wanting to take a boat back and find the truth.

(Dicle: Tigris)

Ancient Byzantine columns had been incorporated into the decorative pillar facade, which used both white limestone and black basalt to bold effect.   Sal said, Look at the frieze of Kufi script carved in limestone. You can see how impressed they were with the ancient Roman decoration.   Irma said, That column has a tessellated carving repeating a Greek cross motif. It was spacious but austere, with no dome. The mihrab was a large cream-colored limestone enclave with band of basalt. It was quiet and pious.   Phim said, Let us ask the Imam to teach us more about Islam.

9 Islamic Prayer

The Imam said, What can I do for you? Phim explained their situation, and asked for explanation about Muslim prayer. The Imam said, Salah (Arabic) which means prayer or blessing (of God) is a pillar of Islam. There are five prayers every day at set times. The ancient model for this came from the Christian monastics (via Gabriel), so you could say that Islam has preserved the ancient emphasis on prayer. We stand, bow, kneel and prostrate. All these are ancient holy attitudes, found in the Orthodox Churches. What do we say? Essentially, praise, bless and ask God for guidance.

The Imam continued. The five prayer times are as follows: the Fajr (dawn); the Zuhr (noon); the Asr (afternoon); the Maghrib (sunset); the Isha (night). In Turkey we translate the names: Sabah dawn, Öğle noon, Ikindi afternoon, Akşam sunset, Yatsi night. We have set times. If you pray with intention, you are in grace with God. You feel good and confident. Islam is closely bound to the cosmic rhythms of the daily rotation of the earth, our orbit round the sun, the beautiful secrets of the stars. We pray as the world turns, in harmony with God's will.

11   St Mary Church

The small Syriac Orthodox Church had
a tiled dome. The altar was separated by
a rail, and there was Islamic influence
with muqarnas. Icons. There were pews.
It was recently restored. Phim sat,
remembering the Armenians in
Jerusalem. In the restaurant nearby, the
chef prepared the lamb ribs with rice,
Kaburga Dolması. A Kurdish feast - for a
special holy day, or for the ancient
Christians a celebration feast. The rib
cage was steamed for hours. The bones
lifted out and the tender meat shredded
over the rice.   Yaeli said, The nomadic
Hebrew and Kurd. How different are
we?

(Diyarbakir)

It was beautiful weather the lake an unusual light blue color. The water is salty and high in minerals, said Mehmet, the fisherman who was taking them to the island. My mother is Armenian and my father Turkish. I'm a Christian but not very religious. Why can't we love one another, like my parents do?   They disembarked and Mehmet led them up to the ancient Church. It was built in 921 when Armenia was still intact as a nation but suffering from attacks on all sides. We are the cross carriers, said Mehmet.

13   Holy Cross Church

It was a Greek cross plan with a conical tower, like the ancient churches in Echmiadzin. Mehmet pointed to the cross Surp Haç, Holy Cross in Armenian. They have a yearly mass now. People come from all over the world. Irma said, Islands were often places of holy sanctuary. They stood in the center, surrounded by tall Romanesque alcoves. Joseph prayed by a modern icon of the Blessed Virgin Mary. It was peaceful. The Van Rock towered above the lake. Listen, said Sudan, the breeze came through the open arch and moved through the church.

Mehmet had taken them fishing. Phim and Irma helped him haul up the nets. Anchored up in the middle of the lake. Mehmet showed him how to gut and prepare fillets. Covered them in flour. He lit a portable gas cooker. Pan-fried in olive oil. Served with cut lemons and fresh bread.   From this morning, he said with a smile. Mehmet opened his cooler bag and pulled out three cans of chilled Efes Pilsen. It had an aquamarine label. The sun was going down as he poured out the beer. Cheers, said Phim and Sal together.

15 Ishak Pasha Palace

They parked the Merc and walked to the palace (1785). It stood on the old caravan route that arrived from the East south of Mount Ararat, commanding magnificent views of the plain. A couple had been allowed to be married there. In the main courtyard a band was playing music, and the bride and groom were dancing. TV cameras were filming. A man explained, The bride's not Turkish. She's a Greek. Where from? They live in London. She's a fashion designer. He's a surgeon. He's a direct descendant of the Ottoman sultans, the Osmanoglu family.

(Dogubayazit)

16   Glaciers

Phim looked at the snapshots of Mount Ararat. What a beautiful mountain. It was an ancient volcano, like Mount Fuji in Japan, rising up majestically from the plain, visible from far away. There was a constant snow cap. It appeared that the glacial ice on the top had been shrinking gradually over the last 50 years. They took it as a sign of global warming. If you raise the overall general temperature of the planet by only a fraction of a degree, enormous changes would occur. If this were true, it would be deep within the task.

17   Signs

God has set his sign in the heavens. Phim had always thought that the beauty of nature was a sign. Mount Ararat was where Noah's ark rested as the great flood began to abate. On the snow cap? Was that why it spoke such a message? Overpopulation, industrial achievement, electric lights burning through the night, decade after decade, little by little the fragile tissue of the world is torn, little by little we lose our lovely home. If we cannot reverse what we have done, then we have to get ready. How can we do that, thought Phim.

18   Volcano

Back to the beginning again. The mountain was at the roots of faith. Fire-storm on the heights, thunder, dinning, lightning flashing. Someone had said that the signs that Moses gave were what had happened when a mighty volcano erupted in that region. He himself climbed a mountain to speak with God. Sinai was a not a volcano but it had been formed by the folding of the earth's crust. Huge cataclysmic forces in the birth of our home, settled into such beauty. The Merc hurried on past brown summer fields. A green olive stood there valiant as ever.

Consider the sound of A-ra-ra-t. A place, a people? Urartu? Hebrew letters teaching God. In Armenian Masis: various suggestions for meaning are offered, "great" or "hero" or "mountain," or "mother," which seems obvious (being a double peak of fertility). For Armenia it represents a nourishing life-force; but not for the Turks, who call it mountain of pain Ağrı Dağı. The Kurds call it fiery mountain. How astonishing that two facets of God are shown, both the beginning and ending. Like the Nile or Jordan, a living natural sign. The greater and lesser peaks look like pillars of a gateway.

Climbing the mountain of ourselves.
Why is it always mountain? The best
explanation all-ready-made. He thought
of the great and good, who'd confronted
the challenge of the age, the 2000 year
gateway. The entrance to the Third
Millennium. Saint John Paul II
struggling up the mountain as he fought
senility. Bartholomew Ecumenical
Patriarch. Queen Elizabeth II, now in
advanced age, still walking onward,
bowed by the years, but by goodness
there was strength to admire. Year after
year sending out the Christmas Message.
Continuance in duty. Phim felt suddenly
guilty.   Well, there it is. Find the
answer.

Saint John Paul II (1920-2005); Bartholomew Ecumenical Patriarch (1940-); Queen Elizabeth II (1926-2022).

Phim had all but forgotten his old English teacher, who'd taken such trouble to get him into Oxford. Classes after hours. Think, Phim. What's the poet really saying. Jim'd written a poem about a mountain. It was a metaphor for old age, for suffering, for everything. Phim remembered the most important lines. They were climbing upward. "Colder and colder, lean on my shoulder." How did it go? Memory. Why don't you work better? He'd been dying of cancer. He'd visited him but the feelings were dead. He'd said, Everything I eat turns to ashes in my mouth.

Phim peered at the google map. How curious. Mount Ararat was there like a mark, placed between the two seas. A beacon. Does it look like a pyramid? In those most ancient days what prompted them to build those pyramid time-tombs? Looking at the maps Phim had thought once that it was all planned to give a message. But accurate maps were a new phenomenon. The land changed. The city moved 10 km inland. Look! Britain is a laughing angel and winged Ireland her cherub together how good. Then Victoria came into his thought. Then he thought about the famine.

23   Dad's Eyes

He'd written a poem about his father's blue eyes. How beautiful they were. It was the pain of not being able to talk to him properly. Why was that, he asked himself. It was some blocked up river, a dam of feeling, he could weep about him, and used to get so angry with him, mighty insolent fury when he hurt Mum, they slung missiles at each other, and Mum would crumple into tears again. Little man Phim all of six years old. Dad drinking whiskey again watch out. O how his eyes changed into terrible eyes.

He imagined himself climbing the mountain, as he would in a few days. I hope I'll be able to. Then the darkness came to him, in a deep swirling fiercely cold wind, and he remembered what he had felt before. An idea to help you understand. The dementors have invaded your story and destroyed your patronus. Lift up your precious tender memories and see how they crumble to dust in your hands. Iscariot? See your Mum and Dad. How they look like me. It was the Locust chattering with his mandibles on Phim's wheat-green head. I am you.

25   Dad Suffering

Phim struggled to make sense of his schooldays, thinking about his father, trying to grasp hold of a warm and loving memory. He saw him again, holding up his hand, puffy with arthritis, and wincing in pain, and he limped up the mountain of his life, carrying Phim's large school trunk on his shoulder. Am I dreaming again, Phim groaned, not daring to tell his Dad who was dead that he had felt aggrieved and bitter, driven by it to study hard. Why can't I find some happy memories? He shook his head. They wanted you to be happy.

Handsome and strong, clever and witty, cruel and how he enjoyed the cruelty, hello Phim he said, and hit him again. Phim bore it. Not admitting to himself that he loved him. He admired him. He wanted to be loved, that was it, wasn't it. You let it happen for that. You loved him and hated him. He was so infinitely higher. He was a dark-haired Greek god. I was a serf. I envied his beauty, his cleverness. A flash of self-understanding broke through. I never dreamt about him like that — but I did have fantasy dreams.

27   School Rebel

The task had become his life. In a few days they'd be on the mountain. His atheist phase. Age 17. He stood in the chapel. Bravely refusing to sing the hymns. Because it was not free-choice. It came from them. He didn't know how influenced he was by them. It seemed brainless now, older and wiser. The hymns were beautifully written. Exclusive claims on truth are made by each one of us within a short space of time. Only a few generations. All before are wrong. All after are wrong. Brave Phim not singing, "Come down O Love Divine."

The mistake he had made was to think that he could have been happy on his own, even though he had in fact been quite happy, surging up out of the crystal water of the Mediterranean after swimming in flippers, skimming the sand, and chasing the bright fish. Swimming on his own in an epiphany of peace, look up at the surface, there were angel voices blond-haired brown-eyed singing in joyful strength, if only he could hear the truth, the beauty that you feel is the key to the task you will be given.

Face the task: to find God to hold to, the source of strength, strong enough to burn away the nightmare. Step by step on the road of his life, more and more broken-hearted, have I lost all feeling? Age 12. Visiting the hospital when Mum had a nervous breakdown. Can I remember it properly? Hard, cold, wiped out, it was numb. Don't tell anyone. Blame her? Dad's fault. A little boy, as he thought himself, I want Mummy to love me, but she's gone mad. Daddy's angry all the time. Whispers dark to take the step.

More memories came back to him. He visited his sister when he was at university. She was having a difficult time at her college. Her relationship with her flat-mates. Her boyfriend. There was so much unhappiness. He sent her poems and she wept at them. She praised him. She wept so much. She encouraged him. Dead in his feelings or unable to respond properly. O what was wrong. Once she had said, Do you never think of me, Phim? You are totally self-absorbed. I didn't do what I was supposed to do. I was never self-sacrificing for anyone.

There was more, much more, flooding into his mind, more than he could bear at this moment, it was too much. He stumbled forward into the shadow, getting ready to leave. Stop, Phim. His sister's boss in the London welfare place she hinted about what he did to her. There were other dark memories he could not hold onto, what happened to Mummy, I hear her shrieking at Daddy. There was so much anger in him he could burn up the world. Climb Arara and let the fire run out into the sky; the Sun good friend you'll help.

They were now approaching Doğubayazıt where they would join the tour and set out for the base camp. There were villages. From ancient days many straggling lines of people had passed through, harried by horsemen. An unconnected vision came to him of a mountain village far away. There was a farmhouse. The years fled by. The old wooden temple stood there, empty now, the tiles missing. A church had been built. Phim walked through the vision and learned where love had lived. There the mountain stood. Seedtime and harvest. The Lord loved the good.

33   Learning

Do I have to learn this over and over,
thought Phim, realizing that he had
somehow forgotten what he was just
remembering. There were a lot of facts
that lie buried or hidden from view.
Truth - the evil they did (our anger);
what we actually did to the prisoners
(worse - not told). How the little one felt
when he served a terrible task in the box.
We know about plunder, book-burning,
library-burning, demolition. We know
what they did to the rood screen.
Audrey's shrine. The Muslim died to
save the Christian. The Hindu friend
died for me.

He remembered when he learnt the word "hell." His friend had whispered it. Not allowed to speak it. Age five. A large gully filled with dry leaves they jumped into. Drop a match. As he looked at Ararat out of the Merc, he thought of the old Chinese emperor forced to endure a life of humiliation after the revolution. How intensely bitter had been his suffering and yet, compared to the cup taken by the West African on the slave ship and later, it had been pleasant. What was the point we had to learn?

35   Make It Better

After it was over, thought Phim, what remains, after the weeping alone in my bed. Not capable of thinking about anything except the early cry against his father, it's so unfair, and the stone-cold reply, life is unfair, get used to it, goodbye. Who said that? The answer, said the angel, is in your own nature, when you know the meaning of 22. By supreme intelligence Gabriel came into Mary in Mark, to make it better. Olden ways had gone bad. We must see the bigger picture. Happily the neophyte swept the cedar planks, on a day in mother's love.

Beginning to bite, there was not enough air. Irma, are you all right. She was bent over, moving slowly. Phim thought again of Bridget, and his memory slipped sideways to Tib in Portugal, and dreams of married life, waking up beside her in the morning, waiting outside when she gave birth, no, he would ask to be present, and the baby boy with blue eyes, she had recovered so quickly and she looked happy. It had gone so well he couldn't believe it, and dreaming of it, saw himself on his knees thanking God.

There were no trees. It was scrubby hard tussocks. Already they were 2500 m high. It was hard work. There were horses and donkeys carrying equipment for the first camp. Sudan, who was easily the fittest, moved up to them and started chatting to the donkeys. They appeared to brighten and looked around. It was hard for them, but they were used to it. They were lean and strong and their coats shone. Sudan said, They look after the animals for the photo-shoots. Irma, if you hold onto the harness he will pull you along.

The first camp. They arrived late afternoon. The tour people helped put up the tents. They organized the kitchen area. They ordered tea and baklava, (requested by Phim) the sun westering over the hazy plain. Large mugs of English tea, Turkish milk, two sugars please, sang out Phim. Feeling happy the climb was over. Irma looked drawn. Joseph also. Sal and Sudan much as usual. Yaeli, sitting next to Phim, was radiant. Pray, Phim, this is covenant mountain. The last rains. The rainbow stood over the Holy Land. God bless Mount Ararat a temple to him, she said.

39   First Night on Ararat

Green tent with thin membrane, double
strength down sleeping bags. Two per
tent. Phim sharing with Sal, Jo with
Sudan, Irma with Yaeli. Freezing cold,
they put the lights out at nine. Phim's
thigh muscles aching. Sal said, Wake
before dawn and watch it rise 5.40. Sal
asleep, deep breathing. He'd wake in a
moment. Phim instantly deep into
dream. It was a song with Mum. The
animals went in two by two. Hurrah,
hurrah. A small blue gramophone record.
They walked up the plank. The
Wildebeest said, Weather's bad, Phim.
Too much demn rain.

(Ralph Richardson. *The Story of Noah*. HMV 1960)

Dawn. The second day.   Sal said, We're going up to 4200 m, spend some time, and descend. Night 2 at 3100 m. Day 3 to 4200 m, pitch camp, sleep, push to the summit from midnight Day 4.   They were on the south side and could not see the eastward views, but the light was in the sky, rose to gold. Wind in the ears. Phim sat enjoying the warmth of Sal's presence, he felt safe with him. He could say anything. He was so clever and so strong. But Sal was worrying. There were other tours on the mountain.

Day three returning to the second camp 4200 m. Is there no strength in the air? Phim enwrapped in himself, solipsistically thinking, myself, my life — self-centred in his own ego, not able to think about Sal or Irma or Yaeli or Sudan or Jo. Did he really care about anyone at all? Stop this pain, stop this blinding headache. This is too hard. Let it finish. Why don't they stop for a moment and rest. Why do they always treat me like a fool? Round and round in stupid circles his mind went on.

Midnight. Day four begins. It was bitterly cold. The sky dark so that the stars could shine more brightly. There was wind at the tremendous height but there was also clarity. David a wise little boy stared at the heavens and started his astrophysicist journey. I'm with him, thought Phim, naming a star for himself, a Semitic word نعم na'am, look how bright and good, how far out of reach. Eyes, nerves, brain receive the star-light. Irma said, Look, Orion is up. The three belt-stars. Joseph said, They're called Tres Marias. Sal said, Look, there's the sword.

(Meaning of "na'am" yes Arabic)

Six hours to the summit they said. High altitude headache. They all had it. They had painkillers and water. Phim took a couple. Thudding headache. Follow the one ahead. Nothing to do but follow. Phim was carrying water for Yaeli and Irma. They wore head-lights. It was hard. Pull the air into the lungs. Crampons on. Use the pick. Practice technique. Phim as usual the clumsiest. The wind was very strong indeed. There were no clouds. It was minutes to the top. They linked arms and huddled. Stars above. Looking east. Sunrise! Yaeli say the word, Toda, Adonai.

Weary beyond belief, immense care was needed on the steep snow section. Then it was care not to trip on rocks, knees cracking into deep descent. Dad sang as he did the washing up. Lili Marlene. Mum glimmered in fury. They were angels in his head. They'd fought one another. They were happy again later. Both melted into a dream saying, What have you done with my Lord. La Madeleine in imagination sitting in the garden. Or was it himself, boy and girl, as he must be, thinking, Can I now remember you? How much your love must have been?

45   Turkish Hot Spa

Phim, Sal, Sudan and Jo sat in the huge tub of steaming water. Phim rested his head on the edge and let his legs float. They'd had the Turkish massage. The thigh muscles and calves ached; the back muscles groaned but the heat was seeping in. There was a deep happiness, not unconnected to the four of them together, the achievement of Ararat, and the understanding that had come to him. Who was it that had told him once long ago that hot water was like love? Lying immersed in it, buoyed up in it. He stretched out his legs.

As the Merc moved west, the late afternoon sun flooded the car. Phim sat in the front next to Sudan driving, shielding his eyes. He stared out the window as they headed north. There was a hawk or an eagle in the distance. I wonder what it is? Can we stop a moment? I'd just like to see if I can recognize that hawk.   They stopped. Phim looked through the bins. It was a brown eagle, soaring over the plain. Phim said, I think it's a golden! My first! Irma said, Don't point the binoculars at the sun, nitwit.

Phim stood and imagined the scene. Music sounded from the walls, and chanting filled the cathedral, resplendent with vestments and icons. Candles glittered from every alcove. Monks intoned with deep voices as the patriarch placed the jeweled crown on the head of the young King Hovhannes-Sembat (1020-1041). A shout went up. Trumpets blared. The brass voices remained for a moment in the mind, and faded, and the cathedral darkened. Phim heard harsh cries. Repeatedly the evil came, war brought by so many armies. Plunder and ruin. A piercing sorrow came to him.

(Adapted from John Marinner. *Trebizond and Beyond.* (London: Hart-Davis, 1969) 152-160. See http://www.virtualani.org/)

The Manuchihr Mosque was said to have been the first mosque built in Anatolia by the Seljuks. There'd been some restoration. Had it been adapted from a church? The ancient churches and mosques were very similar. The octagonal minaret was still standing. The Kufi script said, Bismillah - In the name of God. From the Mosque archway, Irma gazed on the gorge that divided Turkey from Armenia. The Akhuryan river was pale blue. How beautiful, look Phim. Sudan said, It's unspoilt. There are trees by the water, said Sal. Yaeli said, Rebuilding that bridge would be a good thing to do.

They took the Merc north of Ani, and parked, and walked over the new footbridge, and entered Armenia. There was a bus service from Kharkov to Norshen. There was horse-riding and agriturismo. Vines on the slopes. A field with a goat. They found a small inn. They ordered khurjin, a traditional shepherd's dish made by the wives. Lamb, onion, bell peppers and tomatoes baked in a lavash sack, the local flatbread.   Armenian pasty, cried Phim, slicing it open. They celebrated with oak-aged Armenian red. Phim drained his third glass and started to sing. Have pity! cried Irma.

In a Kars restaurant, Yaeli noticed awards on the wall. The owner explained, I won prizes for being a woman entrepreneur. Being a businesswoman in traditional society is still difficult. I broke the mould, and built this from scratch, starting with knitting, and then renovating old Russian buildings, and developed a restaurant business. Armenian-Turkish roots. A challenge to make friends and succeed. I went and talked to farmers, sourced the best products, and even made the restaurant famous for goose. It was the first time Phim'd eaten roast goose. Excellent. She laughed. The best in Turkey. Free-range!

Phim looked up at the twin minarets on the madrasa. They were adorned with blue-tiled muqarnas, similar in color to the Mosques of Isfahan.   Heaven in the height, said Sal.   Joseph said, Built by the Seljuks (1265) just before the Ottomans arrived.   Phim asked, Why two   towers?   No   balcony   for   the muezzin?   The   tiles   spiraled   upward making a beautiful pattern. Are these symbolic   columns?   Muhammad   and Ali?   Sudan said, The scholarship of Greece and Rome? Look how the gate has five elaborate stone-carved borders, each different. Are those grapes of joy? An illuminated page in a holy book.

(Erzurum)

Irma said, On the right side of the door
you can see the double-headed eagle
which they've taken from Byzantium.
The tree of life is growing out of the
crescent moon and open-mouthed
snakes or dragons beneath. There are
eight palms and I can see doves.　Phim
said, It looks like native Turk, Islam and
Greek together. It appears that the
dragon is an ancient Turkish motif. The
dragons of the Far East, auspicious,
ferocious, protecting powers.
Anglo-Saxons had similar motifs (Sutton
Hoo) and King Arthur inherited the
name from the Roman Standards,
dragons like angels.

(Erzurum)

The father of the café owner invited them to visit. Here we are. It was a small homestead. Red and blue wooden panels. We've been here for centuries, he said, in English. I worked in a Welsh farm. Ten years. Goat's cheese. Our family's always had goats. He wore a red shirt, bald head, round belly, warm eyes. Are you hungry?   They sat on the wooden verandah and he cooked eggs with sprinkled cheese. Boiled greens. The bread was supple and fragrant. Pomegranate juice. Joseph asked him about Wales. Raw milk cheese. I knew something so I got the job.

(Erzincan)

He explained. Raw goat's milk is heated, curd produced, allowed to drain, stand, formed, and placed into a salted goat's skin to ripen for six months at cave temperature. Taste some. Ripe smell and creamy tangy flavour. Look. Here's a cleaned and salted skin sown into a sac. The moisture slowly moves through the skin. The cheese hardens. The bacteria thrives. They say that this was how cheese began. There are many caves in Turkey.   Phim said, Polyphemus! Was it originally Greek? Can I hold it?   It smelt goaty.   Hey what's that.   There were gurgling bubbling voices.

(Erzincan)

55   Bear-Zoo

Phim had discovered that the Turkish Government had built a natural sanctuary, occupying a wooded mountain valley, at a height of 1200 m. It had been enclosed with high technology fencing, and held a family of brown bears. It was the first "natural" bear-zoo of its kind. It would preserve the brown bear in a quasi-natural environment, and be used for sensitive research into all aspects of flora and fauna. Visitors would see what was happening through special cameras. Some were online. Russia and other nations were cooperating to build a network of natural bear-zoos.

(The Bear-Zoo is still fiction.)

The Bear-Zoo centre was like a university with different sections. In the bear section, all aspects of the bears were studied and monitored. The current topic was the relationship between "natural" diet and the digestive tract. How did the bear succeed so well in building body weight? There was detailed information about the many different kinds of bacteria, some of which were found also in man. The bears were tame and had a happy environment, and were allowed to potter about the large enclosure mostly undisturbed. Ah, said Sudan, if only we'd been able to build such sanctuaries earlier.

In another section of the centre, they focused on the different plants found in the mountain valley. The idea was to have a total picture of the environment, and try to create an island of native species, like a living store-house. They were looking at fungi and bacteria found in the valley soil. What affected which organisms? Different trees favoured different fungi and bacteria. Detailed study of decomposition and healthy forest soil. The centre also formed part of the scientific education of Turkish children, who studied the bears. Birth, raising the bear cubs, following the mother around the enclosure.

The director was a woman, called Lalam Osman. She had studied in Jersey with Lee Durrell. Phim said, It must have been a tremendous struggle to get this going. It was, she said. We had to convince everyone. Then the funds we needed were unbelievable — in the end, it was a huge international cooperation. European nations, Canada, Japan, Russia all gave millions. Sudan said, This is a new step for humanity. We have moved forward as guardians of our world and its creatures. It was what God wanted us to do.

59   Other Bear-Zoos

Lalam said, There are in fact other Bear-Zoos but they were built on different principles. You have the national parks of the US and Canada, where the bears are free to roam. Japan has the Shiretoko Peninsular, a national park. Korea has Jirisan National Park. Our concept is to give the bear freedom to move about, to enjoy the natural smells of the forest, and to be mostly free from human encounter. A special kind of scientific oasis. No risk because of the high security fencing. Compassion for this fellow traveller on planet earth as they enter near-extinction in wild habitat.

As they drove away, Phim searched for more information about bears in the Balkans, and found an old clip about a dancing bear. In the city square, a keeper was tethered to the bear, which was muzzled, and which stood on its hind-legs dancing unsteadily around him. It was a huge brown bear. He looked in reasonable condition. How many aeons humanity had co-existed with you. Once plentiful in the northern regions, now almost extinct. Can we at least allow you these happy gardens to live in, rather than cold concrete and gawping crowds?

I will not judge you as a church, or even as a faith, or a people — I will judge you as a species, says the Lord. That was the great teaching held by the Jews and transmitted to the world in Genesis. Sudan continued, The green call to Islam. I call you from the desert. Prosper my children. Become scientists. Wear green in my honour. The human race must treat the world as a garden, not a plunder-box. While the nations stockpiled nuclear arms and expensive fighters, how many forests were destroyed? Who will love my gift?

62   Tulum Bagpipe

There was a concert of folk music in
Ayder, one of the villages. They parked
the Merc and walked to the marquee.
There was a stage with a tulum player,
and rows of collapsible chairs. They
bought tickets and a glass of beer, and
sat down. The bagpiper began. Was he
tuning up? Phim felt a curious wriggling
movement inside his ears as the
bagpiper ascended and descended the
scales. It was extremely itchy. Then he
launched into a reel. The men sang out.
Now he felt it in his toes. He stood up.
Are you dancing Phim, asked Sal.

(Tulum [sheep] skin, a word for bagpipe)

63   Kaçkar Dance

In the open area outside the tent a circle of dancers had formed, holding hands. Mostly tourists, directed by local people. Sudan, come on, let's join them, said Yaeli, and they linked hands. Irma said softly, Ange be with us. The circle went round. It was joyful. Who were they? Tourists from Istanbul and Moscow. Saudi Arabia and Egypt. Some Brazilians. A few Germans. From inside the tent five bagpipes wailed. Phim waggled his foot outwards and hopped on the other, and then reversed. It caught on, and one by one everyone was following him. A new dance!

They had driven the Merc up to the high pasture Layla (summer village) where the local Hemshin people spent the summer, harvesting the grass for hay, and making butter and cheese from the rich milk. There were two old women sitting on the porch. Phim said, Hello! They smiled back. The guide invited them to walk to the mountain slope above. This is 2000 m. It was now September. Beautiful afternoon. Growing chill. Glorious alpine views. Irma said, It reminds me of Heidi, except these are cows. Large-eyed beautiful animals, they ambled homeward with grace.

They booked into a small pension and planned to spend the day walking in the woods. Nearby, there was a narrow pedestrian bridge slung over the river, which was in spate from the unseasonal rains. They filed over. Phim and Yaeli stood in the middle. The bridge swung gently over the roaring water. It was almost too loud to talk. The spray from the rocks made a fine mist. Phim stared into the churning rushing stream. What a grand noise, shouted Yaeli. They stood and listened. Beautiful leaping spirit, said Phim, looking at shapes moving in the water.

Walking on the trail, early morning, the air moist and chill. It was a section of replanted forest, restoring diversity to the valley with a greater variety of trees. Many slopes had been planted with fir. Towards the Black Sea they grew tea. There were long strands of green moss, and a warbler flitted about the copse, presumably en route to Africa. He stood on a high twig. He sang briefly.   Sudan said, They don't usually sing on migration. That's a whitethroat. A pleasant scratchy chirrup. Doo-doo-doo-dee-dee-diddli-diddli.   Phim said, Bravo! Encore!

Sudan said, I would have thought it was unusual to find a whitethroat in these high valleys. Perhaps he was breeding further north in open country and is on his way south. He showed himself briefly, the white feathers beneath his pointed beak fluffed out like a beard, a brown-grey head and a beautiful round intelligent eye.   Phiiim-phiiim-phiiim-diddly-doodly, he wheezed. Winter will be sunny. Lots of bugs. Liillaallii! Phim chuckled and said, He'll enjoy the annual African insect-feast.   Irma said, What a lovely bird. I hope we'll see some more.

(Sylvia communis)

They climbed up through the forest. Phim at the back, peering about with his binoculars. What's that over there? There was a large dark shape half-hidden behind a shield of dense copse. Phim stopped to look, and the others carried on up the path. The dark shape moved out from behind the shrub and turned towards Phim. It was about 20 m away. With a sudden jolt of surprise and fear Phim realized that it was a large brown bear. The bear moved more quickly, snuffing the air. Without thinking Phim fled down the path.

The bear galloped after Phim. The path descended to the suspension bridge which they had crossed not long before. The bear was rapidly gaining. Phim heard Sudan shout, Play dead, Phim. The bear paused for a moment. From behind him, Sudan, Sal and Jo were approaching. Phim trusted to his heels, and flew along the path, reaching the bridge. He ran over it. The bear caught up. He stood up and grabbed the side of the bridge, and shook it. The bridge undulated violently, and Phim held onto the wire-struts for dear life.

Phim unable to go forward or back, the planks cracking and the bridge twisting and bucking as the bear heaved on the wire-supports. Phim was thrown upwards, clinging on desperately. But now the others had arrived, and the bear abandoned the bridge and disappeared into the forest. Sudan called out, You OK Phim? Shaken to bits, he cried, but OK. Holding on, he tottered slowly back. Sal said, You're supposed to play dead, Phim. Sudan said, I think with that bear Phim took the wiser option. Can you continue? Yes, let's carry on, said Phim.

There was a wire slung across the ravine. They strapped you in a harness and you sped over. Far below the river ran swiftly between the rocks. Who's going first?   I am, said Yaeli, totally fearless.   They strapped her in, and she whizzed over, crying out, Yerushalayim!   The others followed. Phim was reluctant. But there was no other easy way to cross.   OK, strap me in.   A young Turkish woman with strong shoulders and beautiful black eyes buckled him up and smiled. Phim forgot his troubles, and thinking what a smile sped over the water.

Phim and Sal looked at the church from 50 m away. Phim said, It reminds me of Renaissance churches that I visited once in Milan. A Romanesque perfection. Sal said, The roofs are angled and proportioned in a most pleasing way. Clouds or wings or waves? It must have been restored, said Sudan. Looking at the elegant double column facade, said Phim, you can see the new stone. The Trebizond eagle stared towards the right. Inside the church, the frescos under the dome were vivid streams of color flowing from the Gospel. The multiple seraphim wings swirled.

(Hagia Sophia Church, Trabzon)

Christ Pantocrator blessing from high above the apse. Phim craned his neck upwards, the vertebrae grumbling. The paint had faded, but Christ could be seen, his hand raised. He floated within a light-blue ethereal sphere. His robes shone with a dull fiery orange. The halo was reddish gold. Yaeli said, Irma, I love this icon. Phim said, Spirit pours down upon us in warmth and forgiveness. Irma said, It's more holy for not being repainted. Joseph said, The peasant looks up, cries out in love, and stores the image to return to in his daily work.

(Hagia Sophia Church, Trabzon)

74   Ice Dancer

Why are you staring so hard at your iPhone, asked Irma.   Phim said, International Ice Skating.   It was the dancer from Japan. She was trying to surpass the Russian. Phim was entranced. She'd chosen a high wailing song, which sounded like it could have been either Byzantine or Turk. As he watched her, he became her, alone on the ice, leaping up and revolving.   A joyful lamb or kid in springtime.   She span perfect figures, and made a tulip, round and round she flew, an orbiting planet, and looked toward Phim with a flowering face.

(Winter Olympics 2022 宇野昌磨・坂本花織・宮原知子・三原舞依・樋口新葉)

Touring the Mosques in the old city, Phim said, These were all Komnenoi Churches. They remained in good condition. Under the carpet were ancient mosaics, and under the plaster, images. How much Greek blood remained in Trabzon? It was a long history before 1461. 2000 years? Greek colony, ancient gods, Persians, Romans, Ottomans. They sipped a lemonade in Boztepe. Jo said, What a view. The whole city could be seen, the harbour arms reaching out to welcome the ships. Sal said, The guide talks about high-school study-exchange. Trabzon with Cusco and Xi'an. What a good idea. Compare and contrast.

The guide explained, The Turkish tea industry was developed and encouraged by Ataturk. Coffee was favored before. It'd become popular in Islam after they discovered it being drunk in Ethiopia. The Ottomans developed coffee production. Why did we grow tea? The Japanese, and also British friends, told us the climate and humidity in this region might be perfect. A new industry and a national drink. The tea bushes flourished. The industry took off in the 1950s, and tea drinking became very popular. Today, we are a leading world-producer. Nowadays they say that tea is better for the long-term health.

77   Tea & Coffee

We drink the tea in these special tulip glasses. Small elegant glasses show the colour of the tea. It still looks beautiful and exotic to us. Coffee was the old corrupt past. Tea is milder in its effect; coffee accelerates the thought, but brings a downer after. Coffee is good for creative work and passing exams; tea is better in family life, for women, who may be at risk.   Phim said, My friend could not drink strong coffee. It made her hyperactive and then depressed. But I find ideas zip along much better. I do pay for it later, though.

Phim gazed in wonder. It made a colossal din, but what astonishing cleverness. The tea was rolled, fermented, dried, moved along the conveyer belt, and poured into sacks. Carried to a separate shed, the tea was fed into a hopper. Paper cartons were printed, opened, filled, sealed and wrapped in cellophane. One by one they trundled along the belt, were plucked up and placed in the box for export. Fifty shining red packets of best Rize black tea. Imagine how long it would take to do that by hand.   Here you are, said the guide.   Ooo thank you, said Phim.

Sal read from the guide. The monastery stands at the head of a valley with fir-clad slopes. It's been restored. The most remarkable feature is the curtain of white masonry that rises from the rock-base, containing four stories of monk's rooms, standing high above the wooded slope and valley, like an eagle's eyrie. It has a red tile roof. Behind this building are hidden the other monastery buildings, including the chapel. The outside of the chapel is plastered with saints, fresco-icons guarding the sanctuary. In this remote place icons survived the centuries of hostility very well.

Look, said Irma, pointing to the chapel, a cherub with wide-awake eyes and wings of flame flew beneath Christ. Another stared boldly into the future, shouting God's message of peace. The monastery was originally founded to protect a holy icon of the Blessed Virgin. The rock, the mighty bones of the earth, the ancient name of the father, the mountain itself housed the Holy Virgin with Christ in a sacred cave. All the ancient oracles gathered into one with the birth of Christ. Here is a sacred spring, said Yaeli. Phim said, How splendid that it is being restored.

In 2010 the Turkish Government had allowed the Orthodox Liturgy to be sung, the first since the Monastery had been abandoned in 1923, when the Greek and Turkish populations were separated. Sudan said, I can smell the fire that lay between the two parties, Church and Islam. Sal said, May it be forever put out. Irma said, Let God rain mercy upon us all. On his iPhone Phim watched the famous liturgy being sung. The camera showed the soft features of Theotokos on the wall. Patriarch Bartholomew lifted up his gentle voice. Holy Greek words echoed in the courtyard.

As they stood admiring the chapel, a rope dropped from above, and two huge bearded men slid down and grabbed Phim. They ran off to the right, scaling the wall. They strapped Phim onto their back and moved across the cliff. They were soon were lost to sight. Sal and Sudan had been unable to stop them. They started to climb after them. It was precipitous. Phim had a grandstand view, his stomach churning with terror, the fir trees far below. They arrived at an exposed spur, and tied Phim spreadeagled onto the rock.

One of the men operated a drone. It carried a lance with a blade. They brought it up to hover level with Phim, visible to the others, who couldn't see Phim. Phim saw what was going to happen and started to struggle violently. To no avail. They plunged the lance towards him. He roared as it stabbed him, his blood flowing. Sudan followed by Sal were approaching. Sudan took off his belt which had a brass buckle. They turned the drone-lance towards Sudan. He was watching and struck the lance with his swung belt, and it crashed below.

Yaeli was climbing quickly. She was surprisingly nimble and moved up the cliff face above the men. They were about to dispatch Phim. From above Yaeli hurled a rock and one of the men fell down the cliff. She hurled another and knocked him out. He slumped beside Phim. Sudan shouted, Bravo Yaeli! They untied Phim, who was bleeding, and very carefully guided him back to safety. Fearful moments. He'd been lucky again. They'd missed the organs, but it would require hospital. After thirty minutes the Turkish police took them away by helicopter.

Phim lay on the hospital bed, dazed by what had happened, his mind slipping in and out of consciousness. The Trabzon doctor (from Istanbul) and nurses (local) were good. Mist in the fir clad valley swirled into darkness within his mind, a nightmare returning, blaming his own birth and past, a darkness wanting him not to be born. So much to know, when it was known, too much to sorrow. The ancient opponents each carried burdens of suffering impossible to tell. Where to find healing. The Trabzon nurse said, Rest Phim, heal. The doctor has mended you well.

Ancient tombs, the Greek Pontic rulers c. 400 BCE. Carved into the rock. One was more ornate, imitating the pediment of a Greek temple. Another was a round arch and a square hole. Using the iPhone as a torch, they stepped in. Sudan said, I feel something. Joseph said, Pontus is an important connection. There were empty tomb holes for the bodies. Phim said, Grief. Irma said, How ghostly cold it is. She started to sing. Peace to the souls of those who sleep. Her voice filled the tomb. She sang with the Greek word Eirene.

(Ünye. Jn 14.27)

The guide explained. This coast was colonized by ancient Greeks. It remained an island of ethnic Greek culture, while the Persians, Alexander's army, Romans, Byzantines and Turks took control.   Joseph said, Ethnic groups struggle to maintain identity. Often the cost is high.   Yaeli said, Same old problem. Ancient roots and identity. Diaspora and nostalgia.   Sudan said, Tell me about the Pontus.   Phim said, The impossible task, if we think about the length of the human journey, you become me, and I become you.   Sal said, Deepest wisdom and deepest love. Who can achieve such a miracle?

Joseph said, In ancient days Colchis (Georgia) was famed for its riches. This is shown in the story of Jason and the argonauts, who sought the Golden Fleece. Colchis was the sea-limit of the East, and Gibraltar the West. Prometheus was chained on the Caucasus, above Colchis. Phim said, Empires come and empires go. Each required its peoples to wear different robes. But if I loved my old robes, what could I do? If I loved my family and people, and could look after them better, then maybe it was God in me again and again in that choice.

The Pontic tombs faced south. The pamphlet said, The mirror cave, about a kilometre from the main tombs, has a coloured painting showing the Virgin Mary and the Apostles. Had it served as a secret church? A guide offered to show them the way. They walked up through orchards of cherry trees on the slopes. The hillside was filled with grey limestone outcrops. Viewed up close, the rock tomb was monumental. A smooth facade carved into the rock. It was called the Mirror Cave because this facade flashed upon the city when struck by the sun.

Phim squeezed through the narrow
passage on the right of the tomb. It was
a small square cut chapel hollowed from
the rock.   There was no way into the
tomb except through the small square
window on the facade. Was the interior
hollowed out from this entrance?
Impossible labor. Phim stood on Sal's
shoulders and peered into the tomb. A
square chamber. He shone the iPhone.
No fresco of Mary? He listened and
heard his heart-beat fill the space.
Da-dun. Da-dun. A memory-dream fled
by. He could hear the Yeshilirmak far
below, flowing steadily on.

Sal said, You get a feel for the layers of history. A mosaic with a flourishing tree. Ancient wooden doors with beautiful Arabic patterns. Irma paused at a blackened mummy, the concubine of the Bey (14th century).   Sudan said, They say the same thing.   Phim said, Look at this statue. The Hittite storm god, Teshub or Tarhun. How many figures like him could we have met, if we'd been paying attention?   Joseph said, Deus. Ancient Indo-European roots.   Yaeli said, Tanrı. The blue heaven god of the ancient Turks.   Irma said, Look, she prays, Be merciful, Lord, be kind.

They walked over to the cafe and sat inside watching a woman making Turkish meatballs. What are they called in Turkey, asked Phim. Yaeli laughed, You're happy now. You've got meatballs. Irma said, You should have seen the greed when we first had meatballs. He took twice his share. With permission, said Phim, I did ask. Sudan said, Meatballs are bad. We should eat veggie-balls. Sal grimaced. Phim was watching her knead the bulgar wheat dough into cones and fill with the mince. He felt his saliva loosening up and tried not to gulp too much.

(Ishli Kofta Turkish stuffed meatballs, minced beef or lamb)

The woman said, So you like Turkish food. Let's show him an Ottoman dish. Her husband was the chef. He sautéed tenderloin beef with almonds and added slices of peach and apple. He smiled at Phim, When the husband got called up to the Ottoman army, the wife would make a farewell dish. A cup of grape molasses, a cup of water, granulated sugar, slices of sour-dough bread. Reduce the syrup. Soak the bread slices and simmer, turning them a few times. Slowly they become golden-brown. Sprinkle with ground walnuts. Sweet. It's called "Forget Me Not."

Need an account of what happened in Cappadocia ... Phim read through the guide books and searched the internet. Hittite successors dug caves with iron tools c. 700 BCE. Underground shelters or storage. Prosperous crossroads. Early Christians fled persecutions and took refuge in caves c. 200-300 CE. Monastic communities developed under Saint Basil c. 370. Great saints ruled. The region remained prosperous enough (a trading depot) to support monasteries. Islam on the south border. Refugees. Iconoclasm c. 730-840. Icons hidden in cave churches. Icon-lovers versus Icon-despisers. Christian pilgrim community flourishes c. 1000. Underground developed. Arab raiding parties. Seljuks. Ottomans.

Bright surge of yellow flaming into the balloon. Swelling and lifting. It was a young crowd. Infectious excitement as they left the ground. Phim and Irma were nervous, remembering the last time. There were a hundred balloons filling the dawn sky. A meadow of flowers. Joseph said, A birthplace of faith. Phim peered over the edge, he saw a long line of caravans arriving from all quarters. Unloading, stowing in the caves, bartering, exchanging. Taking lodgings. In the houses saying thanks. It seemed to be an unending festivity. The hills were green. Beautiful horses. An easy place to make friends.

For a time Cappadocia was a mad Christian hive of cave building, under the enthusiasm of the feverish first two centuries c. 400-600 as the faith spread to lower levels in the late Roman class structure - then Islam arrived. Polarization? Why this intense purity drive? Pillar penance? Cave life? Justinian imposed stricter conditions. Be a Christian or else. What were the punishments for refusal? What did they do to pagan priests who refused to give up the old house? Unwanted visions came to Phim again, burning houses, soldiers, martyrdoms. They had made sure that the army became Christian first.

97   Cave Church

It was dry and dusty but it must have been greener long ago. They got out of the car, and walked up to the caves. Karabas Kilise. The big church. There was a Greek sister in black with an assistant making a video record. She said, Look at this. They went inside. The cave-church was barrel-vaulted. Every inch was painted. Saints all around. Family alive with us. She sang in Greek to the Virgin. Her assistant lit a candle. The voice at first dull then it flowered and ran through the chamber like a fiery angel of joy.

(Karabaş Kilise, Soğanlı c. 550 CE frescos c. 1100)

The Greek sister said, The good news is that we have just received funding to restore these caves to what they would have looked like at their best. To give visitors something better to look at. There's also been a strong statement of support from about 5 million Turks, asking that Greeks be allowed to worship in the church caves a few times a year. She smiled. At last faith returns to faith. We can love one another. Irma looked pleased. You could join our team. No, she said, this is my task. Restore the beauty and share it.

The Greek sister said, Come to Goreme ... This is called the Elmali Church (apple) because of the orb held by Archangel Michael. The colours were vivid, light orange-ochre and oxide-red. Saints on every wall. There's Saint John bald-headed. Christ Pantocrator looked from above. They'd blotted out the eyes and forehead. Phim felt a surge of emotion. It seemed such a waste. Beauty in the human form is an allegory of God. Am I a peasant worshipping pigmented stone? Then he thought, It's a warning about what will happen, and felt his forehead.

(Elmali Kilise, Goreme c. 1050 now restored)

There was Pantocrator again. He'd been restored. What's the point? The face I saw in my first steps of faith, whether a child or an adult, nobility, gentleness, compassion, taught by the priest what he could do, he will reach out and heal me, warned by the father not to betray him, he would appear terrible in wrath, as I grow and learn the life and bow my head at wisdom, and feel exalted by the voice of the choir singing like angels, he will continue to look upon me, unchanged as I change, in my journey to meet Him.

(Dark Church, Goreme c. 1100)

The Greek sister showed Irma a pamphlet. No one talks about the love and patience that existed between Christian and Muslim. Look at this ancient Shrine to St Mamas in Aksaray, Gökçe Village. It was a Muslim Tekke and Turbe at the same time. At the Eastern end an altar, on the southern wall a mihrab. Mamas was believed to be a saint of healing for both communities. Visited by local women praying for family. Both authorities were hostile to this kind of sharing, but I feel the Lord is present. Who is preventing us from loving one another?

(Tekke: Dervish Lodge. Turbe: Tomb)

A minibus stopped at the traffic lights opposite the Kayseri cafe, filled with young women in dark-blue track suits. There was a football on the side. The waiter said, Our national team. My sister is a football star. Do you like football? I can sell you a ticket. There's an international match today against Iran. Yaeli said. Let's go. They bought tickets. The teams marched onto the pitch. National anthems. Joseph said, A completely new kind of civilization, in which women can be sports heroes and nobody's hurt. Phim said, I'd like to step back to less aggressive sport.

The Turkish team wore bright red soccer gear. The Iranians wore white track-suits, with hijabs. There'd been controversy about wearing hijab in international sport. It had been permitted. Protect the modesty of the women, thought Phim. Sport was inevitably visual, and a healthy young body generated desire. The Iranians under the white were slim and curvaceous, and the Turks, wearing less, stimulated the instincts. Was it so bad? Should only women be allowed? Prickling in his beard, the mind started running after a longed-for ball - Oooh look at her go! GOAL! Hugs all round. Turks looking grim.

Irma said, We were not allowed to play football at school in Egypt. I remember wishing that it had been allowed. It's really about equal opportunity. If boys can enjoy sport, why can't girls? Yaeli said, Exactly. The Turks were fighting back. A beautiful long cross to the right wing, a flying pass to the left wing, a woman with a brown ponytail sidestepped two Iranians, and neatly put the ball in the top left corner. GOAL! She turned to look at Phim, her face beaming, and did a dance, her two hands up in the air, round and round.

The game continued, fast and furious. It was glorious. There was less body contact compared to the men's game, more sprinting and passing. Phim had taken a fancy to the wing. Right wing Turkey and left wing Iran, standing opposite. They were battling now, took the ball, away she flew, her heels skimming the astro-turf. Tackled, fallen, standing, onto her, retaken possession, dribbling like an angel, round another, shoooot!   Allah! Phim shouted joyfully, Goal! That was football. Pure poetry. Overcome by emotion, Phim stood up and did a little dance in front of his seat. Sit down, said Irma.

The whistle went and the game ended. In a moment of exuberance, she booted the ball up high, and very strangely it hung above the stadium for a moment, like a balloon, and then sloped downwards in slow motion with increasing speed to where Phim and the others were sitting. Phim was not thinking about the ball. He was trying to replay the winning shot. How attractive she appeared as she sped to the goal. Sudan caught the ball with this huge hands, and Sal said, Well saved! Can we keep it?   NO, said the British ref. Return it please.

107 Breath

Phim searched for information about the Three Cappadocian Fathers, who stood at the gateway of Christian faith. Saints Basil of Caesarea (330-379) (Kayseri), Gregory of Nyssa (335-395) (Nevşehir), and Gregory Nazianzus (329-390). Phim had always found small nuggets of gold had given him more strength than any long sermon. Two or three verses gave you all you needed, and you could return to them again and again. Gregory of Nazianzus had said, "We ought to think of God more often than we draw breath." Phim drew in deeply, and thought, "But what is God?"

(Adapted from Gregory of Nazianzus, *Five Theological Orations*. Trans. by Stephen Reynolds, 2011. (pdf) From "The First Oration.")

In *The Life of Moses,* Gregory of Nyssa wrote, "The Divine One is himself the Good whose very nature is goodness. There is no limit to virtue except evil, and since the Divine has no opposite, divine nature is unlimited and infinite. If you pursue true virtue, you participate in God, who is absolute virtue. If you desire by nature to join with virtue, the good being without limit, then your desire to be good will stretch without limit. It is impossible to be perfect. Perfection is God who has no limit." What a happy definition, thought Phim.

(Adapted from St. Gregory Nyssa, *The Life of Moses* [c. 390], trans. Abraham J. Malherbe & Everett Ferguson. Paulist Press, 1978.)

Saint Basil said, "As you take your seat at table, pray. As you lift the loaf, offer thanks to the Giver. When you sustain your bodily weakness with wine, remember Him who supplies you, to make your heart glad and comfort you. Has your need for food passed away? Let not the thought of your benefactor pass away. As you put on your tunic, thank the Giver of it. As you wrap your cloak about you, feel greater love for God."   Food, thought Phim. Number one need. What we cry for first.

(Quoted in Peter Schaff, ed. *Basil: Letters and Select Works*, in *Nicene and Post-Nicene Fathers*, vol 8; from "Homily V: In Martyrem Julittam.")

Nazianzus was exhorting Eunomius (an opponent) to refute the Greek philosophers. "Attack Pythagoras and the Orphic beans, and the "ideas" of Plato and the circulation of souls, attack Epicurus and his pleasure, attack Aristotle, attack the Stoic and the Cynic." Did he mean read, understand and reject?   Or was it a secret reading list for intellectual growth? A thought flashed upon Phim. The same God is alive within these ancient theories, and the Church Fathers' teaching. Alive in contradictions. Eternity is a vacuum; life is the warm sun. Surely we had to find truth in all these gifts.

(Adapted from Gregory of Nazianzus, *Five Theological Orations*. Translated by Stephen Reynolds, 2011. (pdf) from "The First Oration.")

A stern-looking woman was taking notes as an endless stream entered the Kaymakli caves. Are you studying tourists, asked Phim. No, she said, we're the Mediterranean International Tourism Standards Bureau. We visit key sites and make recommendations. How would you judge this place, asked Yaeli. She frowned and said, Cannot say. In many places there are too many tourists. Facilities and information are bad quality. We must have better standards. Think what happens after 50 years of overcrowded visits. As if to illustrate her point, a little boy was carving his name on a wall.

They sat around a cave table, with a trough to put the feet in. A waiter brought them a Turkish tea in a tulip glass, and a dollop of Dondurma ice-cream, which Phim chased around the bowl. They'd covered walls and floors with exquisite carpets, locally made and from Iran. They were selling them. A small fortune. Phim looked at the pattern and tried to find its meaning. A mosaic of squares and triangles forming symbolic flowers, a wealth of colour, larger patterns visible as you stood and gazed. Yaeli said, Feel this one. It is so soft.

113   Rock Viper

Phim wandered off with Sudan to a small dilapidated village. Poverty. Chickens skittering by the half-built yellow limestone wall. Piles of debris from the years. Rusty old farm machines. It seemed deserted. They walked on further and came to rocky cone-pillars. As they climbed higher, Sudan said, It looks like the moon surface. Yellow sand eroded between the pillars. A long snake lay basking on the rock, warm in the sun. Grey with a dark brown zigzag. Large wedge-shape head. The black tongue flicked out, scenting. Sudan exclaimed in joy. Rock viper. Stand back Phim.

(Near Goreme)

Sudan sang softly in Swahili. The rock viper was staring at Sudan's right hand, which had become a rock viper, weaving from side to side. It had beautiful dusky-gold eyes. It slowly uncoiled and moved to Sudan, whose elbow rested on the sandy rock. It looped itself around his forearm, and unlooped. It appeared completely at ease. Phim said nothing, terrified to break the spell. Sudan breathed out a gentle phrase and the rock viper moved away. It moved gracefully. Sudan said, These ancient inhabitants are increasingly rare. Fearsome friends. Wisdom teachers if you could learn from them.

As they walked back to Goreme, Phim thought about the bleak rocky landscape. It had been used in countless films. Was it another revelation of the future, as the Egyptian desert had appeared to be? Phim remembered the old communist teaching about faith. Use it to unite the people, generate a purpose in them, conquer with that overwhelming feeling of righteousness, and then take possession of the land and wealth you desire. Make sure you stay on top; make sure they remain below. Somehow the landscape agreed with the thesis. It's the truth, isn't it? Prove me wrong.

Phim grumbled at himself, seeking an answer to the old problem of the selfish human will, the survival gene, the strongest monkey grabs the nuts, the weaker one, hard cheese. Examples please. O don't let me think it all over again. Joshua, Constantine, Mehmed. What would the highest angel say? Name me the angel of peace. Against the survival instinct we are given the writing and the book. Good law is an angel, isn't it, Phim? Phim looked at the lunar world around. Good law? Ownership and abuse. History of the human race.

When the first human beings arrived here they must have been amazed. Columns capped with hard stone. How to explain them. Hard volcanic surface, softer tuff beneath, eroded by thousands of years. An uncanny ghost town. It must have been greener then.
— Big Man, can we live here?
— No. Mighty Spirits are here. Leave.
— Look, Big Man, cave-home.
— No. Too dangerous.
— Look, a spring. Water. Big Man, let's
     live here.
— Fresh water? OK. Big Man live here.
     You in that cave over there.
Phim wondered what Big Man would have looked like. Undoubtedly hairy-chested. Big muscles.

There was a tunnel branching off the main tunnel. Where did it go? Sal, I'm just going to take a look. It narrowed abruptly. Phim squeezed through, and suddenly felt the rock grip him round the guts. He was caught. Sal! He shouted, I'm stuck. His voice could only just be heard.   Phim! Are you all right, shouted Irma. That'll teach you not to guzzle baklava every time we find a cafe. Yaeli shouted, Thought you'd gotten rather round in Turkey.   Phim said, Cut the cackling!   Joseph said, We're going to pull. Joseph grabbed his legs.

(Derinkuyu)

Joseph heaved on Phim's legs and Phim let out a yell.   Racked for my sins!   Sal joined Joseph and they pulled again. Ow! Phim cried out.   Make yourself thinner, Phim, breathe out. Think thin. Sudan joined in and they heaved, and Phim came free. They all fell backwards in the tunnel.   Thanks, said Phim, feeling ungrateful.   Joseph said, Do you want me to put a chain on you, Phim? Stay close to Sal and Sud. They could have been there waiting for you.   Phim leant against the wall which stabbed at him with a sharp projection.

Descending a long narrow stairway. It opened up into a large cavern. They had arrived at the deepest level. Dug in the floor was a large Greek cross. On the walls there were ancient icons, facing the centre. They'd been restored. Small electric candles glimmered. Basil, Gregory, Gabriel and Michael. Christ with his Mother. An Empress on her throne. Ancient naïf Byzantine style. What are you doing so far underground, thought Phim. It was comfortably warm. The saints swam before him. They stood in the cross. Drowsiness seeped into the cave. In a few moments they were asleep.

As Phim gazed on the icons, Saint Basil detached himself from the wall and appeared to walk towards him. Tall domed forehead, long thin beard, black eyes of wisdom. He looked at Phim with a twinge of annoyance. He said, The manuscript and shard. Philae Isis. Why won't you understand? Birth is rebirth and life is made new. Knowledge must be shielded. Ange died for you. Where are you now? He held up a beautiful book, encrusted with rainbow jewels and stars. The icon-figure wavered and there was a smell of incense.

Now Gabriel stirred, folding behind him his beautiful wings, moving out of the icon towards Phim. Phim was filled with terrible fear, not certain if it were an angel of goodness, or a demon of destruction, fearful that his life would end.   Gabriel spoke, Do not fear Phim. We've come to tell you we love you. You're failing the task. Find an answer in Islam. With your friends, build love for Islam. Do this better, Phim! Go to the throne of the Mother. Learn from Athos and Athens. Gabriel looked at him piercing deep. Such sweet joy came!

The others lay on the floor of the cavern, fast asleep, like a picture from an old story, either of Arthur, or wasn't there something about the seven sleepers? From the tunnel on the right a small hunched man wearing a deerskin round his waist loped in. Matted hair, hairy back. In his hand he held a pointed stone, round at one end, and glittering at the other. He knelt and dug at the floor. He worked furiously and left a mark. He gaped at Phim in a mighty surprise. He looked around and made gestures.

The hairy man looked up and Phim looked with him. The cavern had become a planetarium. There was the humming projector, whirring and clicking, and they were in outer space. Points of light of varying brightness hung all around. Phim winced at the brightness of that one. A small wisp of heat brushed his cheek. His eyes were miraculously clear. He could reach out and touch them, bright cool stones. A cloud of milk in water washed through. Mentally he fought with the gifted beauty to make sense. They were waking. Slowly they climbed the narrow stair out.

There was a fight on the surface. Disagreements. Violent words. *We should not use it.* Someone threw something into the ventilation shaft. Phim and the others were deep underground, at the middle level. He heard it scuttling inside the shaft, and moving into one of the corridors. Then he heard no more. They carried on, shining their mobiles into the dark. It was narrow, only one person could proceed. They came to another cavern and paused. Something the size of a dog scuttled in, and started swelling. Bulbous black abdomen, legs with stiff hair, glinting eyes and clicking mandibles.

Phim! It called out. Phim! Up in front of her, she projected a beautiful face. Phim's rush of fear evaporated. He felt safe and happy. It was his own mother smiling at him. He stepped forward. Sudan yelled, No! Phim, she called again. She was overwhelmingly powerful. Now she threw before her the women he'd loved, Brigid, Tibs, even Irma, Yaeli, Oriel. Phim felt so happy he walked towards her. Now she showed film stars. Julie, Kate, Emma, Nadiya, Helena, Liz. Phim reached towards her in joy. The pictures faded. She scuttled forward. Sudan grabbed Phim and ran.

Sudan shouted, Sal, watch out, poison. Sal stripped off his jacket and threw it over the spider's head. It was now the size of a Saint Bernard. Yaeli, shuddering with horror, delivered a flying kick. The spider became enraged, clicking and spitting furiously. They fled. Sudan and Phim leading. Sal behind. They heard her following, her claws scrabbling on the dusty stone. She was not very quick. Sudan said, Give Sal your jacket. Do not get bitten. It will be death. Joseph stripped off his jacket. They passed it back to Sal.

Sal faced her, seeing his own mother, feeling the unearthly sweetness, longing to go forward to her. Phim shouted, Sal! Watch out. The picture crumbled and there she was, the mobile showed her glittering eyes. There was foam dripping from the points of the curved fangs left and right. Sal flung the jacket over her head. He stamped at her, but it was like steel coils. Her poison burned the fabric. Run, he shouted. They set off again as fast as they could. They heard her again, scabbling in the tunnel, clicking and hissing.

She was unable to move very quickly because of the shape of the tunnel, which was too narrow for her. She had swelled considerably. Phim, she called again. I'm hungry. It was Phim she wanted most of all. She would feed upon him. Up ahead there was a massive round millstone, used for sealing the tunnels. There was a groove. Joseph and Sudan entered the alcove and heaved on the great stone disc and it rumbled home. It could not be moved from the other side. They heard her faintly clicking and scabbling. Let's get out of here, panted Phim.

The icons formed a pictorial tapestry of
the Gospel, including the
Protoevangelium of James. They could
have been used by a holy brother, to
teach the catechumens, or visiting
supplicants seeking a holy cure.
Pentecostal scenes were prominent.
Phim noticed that Christ on the cross
stood with outstretched arms, not
pendent as in Latin crucifixes. A Greek
letter? A glory sign? The altar panels
were splendid, with gold ground, indigo,
yellow, blue and turquoise. The blue
was lapis lazuli, costing a small fortune.
A holy hermit had lived here walled-in,
praying night and day, sanctifying the
place.

(Tokali Church, Goreme c. 1000)

They drove to the Sultan Reed (Sazlığı) Park, south of Lake Yay. The Sultan's old hunting grounds. It was a large wetland, a designated Ramsar site. Phim stood and listened to the breeze softly stirring the stubble. The walkway went through the harvested reed beds, drying out in October. In August they were green whispering walls. There were few birds to be seen. A lonely coot picked his way, unconcerned, his white frontal shield shining. The autumn sun was warm on the weathered decking. A wide open sky. The plain stretched to Mount Erciyes, gently presiding.

They visited the museum, who said, You should come here in April. They had some ancient stuffed birds. They showed a film of a heron with saffron breast-plumage, long striped crest feathers and a sky-blue beak. It raised its crest and puffed out its chest, unthinkingly inviting ancient and modern man to plunder the feathers. Its round eye made it appear bad-tempered. An ancient king aggrieved at the modern world. It caught a fish, and glared at the camera. I came a long way. I've been waiting for the others. Where are they? I want to show them my robes.

(Ardeola ralloides)

Sal had found a Turkish restaurant in a cave, carved in imitation of a Hittite Temple. A toast to Cappadocia past and present, said Phim. Local red wine Öküzgözü (Ox-Eye). In the middle of the room, a young blond woman flung her hair aside and started singing. She flashed a smile at Irma. She danced like a breeze through a poplar tree. What's the song? Phim asked the waiter, who stood listening. She's calling to God, saying, I loved and I lived. She shot a fierce glance at Phim. He felt a flame like whisky run along his nerves.

("I loved, I lived" inspired by song by Ebru Gündeş 2019)

As they drove to Hacıbektaş, the village shrine of the medieval Sufi master Haji Bektash Veli, Phim wondered how different Christianity and Islam really were. Consider the big picture. Constantine was converted when he saw the cross in the heavens. In this sign you will conquer. There it is on the Holy Lamb, the word Nika, the old goddess of victory, Nike. Victory in war. As the Janissaries developed, they adopted Bektash as their official Sufi order. It was abolished when they were abolished, when they'd become an Ottoman millstone. A few catchwords, a strong military bond, on to victory.

Phim visited a Bektashi website and found a teaching. "The heart is the window to the Sovereign of the worlds. Between Allah and all things is a veil, but between Allah and the heart of Man there is none. The heart is like the Ka'bah." Phim thought, God knows the heart. Go to your heart, a holy shrine to God. How will you get there? "The travelling companion is Allah. Love is but Allah's divine kindling. The fireplace of that kindling is the heart of those who have arrived." God helps the heart kindle to be in love with Himself.

(Adapted from text "Maqalat" on website: http://bektashiorder.com/teachings-of-haji-bektash)

Phim read through a Bektashi Catechism they'd posted. It was full of secrets requiring explanation, drawing on both Hebrew and Christian esoteric knowledge, and declaring truths in Arabic and Islamic tradition. Holy numbers and letters, just the same as Hebrew and Christian. Well, thought Phim, if the truth is One, then it is certainly One, and God is God, and He will love you, whatever your language, or theology. As you pray, your body forms the letters of the word Adam. Alif-Dal-Mim. Out of the primate into the human. To be a true person is to love God.

(Responding to text on website. http://bektashiorder.com/a-brief-bektashi-catechism)

Walking to the tomb of the holy saint, there was a crowd of Albanian pilgrims with a guide. For so long associated with Ottoman strength, the order had been exiled to Albania. Phim looked at them, reverently placing their hand on their heart. Most of them women. It was the unity in God at the core, the Sunni and Shi'ite holy ones, Muhammad and Ali united, the loss of ego by true devotion and prayer, Phim felt their warmth and goodness. He glimpsed their families and their love for one another. Complete strangers and a strange feeling of love.

It was among the most memorable Mosques they had visited. Solid walls and large square windows. Plentiful use of beautiful wooden furnishings. It was an older Ottoman style. It had a warm family atmosphere. Holy place of beginning for us. Our hard duty, our victories, thank you God. Bektashis were survivors from an older time. A provincial palace for the saint, simple but strong. Let us follow his good teaching. In the heart of the complex the holy tomb, covered by a light-purple cloth and a shining green cover. The walls were alive with colourful arabesques.

Sudan was telling a story. It was about 200 years ago. God spoke to a scientist in a dream. He told the scientist, Use the most powerful microscope you can find. I want you to examine the smallest building blocks of creation and read what I have written. The scientists used their instruments. No good. Generations went by. Technology improved. They found words and started to decipher them. God had written: Now use an instrument with the opposite power, and read what I have written in big letters. Yaeli laughed, And what did He say?

Phim was reading a newspaper on his iPhone. A young boy in Turkey had made a discovery and they'd put it on the front pages.   Five-year old discovers life!   Sifting the pond water in the middle of Turkey, he'd found some tiny shrimps, about the size of a full stop. There was a picture. An orange rugby ball, with yellow see-through legs. Amazingly, it was a new species. Sudan snorted. Clever little prodigy boy. How wonderful. Draw them and label them. Then what happens? Looks good, doesn't it, but what do you really care about preserving our precious world?

Phim was finding out about stars. There was a tutorial website. As he learned more, all the information they had gathered on the long journey began to piece together into a large mosaic. Look, she said, Apparent magnitude and absolute magnitude. The brightness we can see or the true brightness. She showed pictures of star-sizes. There's our sun. Look. A micro-blip compared to Antares, a red supergiant. The stars change, she said. They expand. They shrink. They burn up. The same laws apply. The same truth. Time is finite. Therefore, love your fellow creature. Love this house.

Phim was in Konya, Akyokuş Park, looking up at the sky with his binoculars. The Pleiades. He counted the stars. Not seven but was that ten? He searched world-wide references. A fisherman had married an angel-princess and gone to heaven. Seven children of Subaru, she said. Time passed slowly there. It was a cluster, k̲îmāh. Not to be counted. Banded together by God. How many? Holy secret. Ancient advice. Sail when they rise; store the boat when they set, storms coming. He looked at them again. Blue-white diamonds set in obsidian. Seven holy maidens with mother.

(Amos 5:8; Job 9:9; Job 38:31. Hesiod, Works and Days. Urashima Taro Fudoki version.)

Islamic study of the heavens was the most pure of all disciplines. The Arab astronomer sought to get closer to Allah by going further than the Greeks. They'd been the best astronomers for 500 golden years. Why did they lose that? The Turks did not favor it. There was something in the ancient Turkish culture which hesitated to seek such holy knowledge. There was the same hesitation in Christian Rome. It was dangerous to delve too deep - it was forbidden. 1610 Galileo looked through his telescope and counted more than we'd ever been told. A door opening.

Phim thought about what science said about stars. For example, the information they gave about the Pleiades was nothing short of incredible. How much one had to take on trust. What if you were blind, and they were just spinning glorious stories about the stars, none of which were true? You'd just have to believe them. Phim remembered the moving incident in *King Lear*, when Edgar in the guise of Poor Tom leads blind despairing Gloucester to the edge of the fictional cliff. Were the stars like that? No, thought Phim. Truth exists. Electric power surges from a nuclear generator.

What wonderful binoculars these are, thought Phim. A bit heavy to lift up, the arms ached after a minute, but the wide aperture let in the light and there they stood, glittering beautiful blue-white beads forming a ladle, begging to be understood as a message of eternal strength. Moving quickly, they stood high above Phim in the heavens. Blasted neck-bones, he muttered, unable to watch for more than a moment. How strange they were there every night, wheeling through the ancient sky, their cool trickles of long-ago light soothing the mind with quietness.

Phim peered through his binoculars at the Milky Way. It was an exceptionally clear night. They had driven out to a hillside, and parked the car.   Is this OK, Phim? said Irma.   Should be.   Stars upon   stars   upon   stars.   The super-telescopes revealed the deep sky objects to be clusters of millions. Where are we   headed?   To become   highly intelligent   and   solve   these   puzzles? Wait, was that an owl?   Unlikely.   It would be so easy to throw out God. The human mind with talons?   On and on?   Emotion-free - without weakness world.   A wren to stand against and trill, No.

Three young Muslim women were walking past the Mosque an hour before dawn, singing as they went. Only their faces visible. They paused for a moment. One of them said something. A peal of laughter. Quickly stifled. They continued singing. Phim, Sal and the others, stood watching them. Yaeli waved at them. Hi! Hello, said one, wearing great round sunglasses, very British accent. We're waiting to say a prayer as the sun rises, standing in this holy place. Same as us, said Irma. Sal said, I'm Muslim. Well, let's share the sunrise, said sunglasses. My name's Ameena.

The sun rose bright yellow filling the empty streets. There were a few people in the square, but it was blissfully quiet. Shall we sing together, said Phim. Fire ahead, said Ameena. Joseph said, I'm a Coptic priest. I'll begin. Please follow. "Thanks be to God. For the gift of life. For you and me. For peace and love. Blessings on your family. By our love for God. By our love for each other. Bless our lives, O God, amen. Allah! Lord God! Thank you, amen." The sun stood and lit the domes; the tiles flashed with a holy flame.

They stood in the porch. There were framed examples of calligraphy. Rumi verses. The Ottoman calligraphic seal. A candelabra of fine glass, with sea-green calixes on slender arms holding translucent tubular flowers, dripping with glass diamonds. They entered the hall. Tombs were cloaked in green, with large white turbans. Writing was everywhere. The walls were filled it. It was a huge family mausoleum. The largest tomb belonged to Rumi. It was a chapel for a beloved saint. Above the tomb, a rainbow of color was woven into beautiful text. Islam!

Phim looked up into the dome, painted in autumn colours. With his bins he could see Arabic letters radiating from the centre, and among the colored leaf and tendrils were leaves with holy text. Phim thought, The world was written by God's finger. He wrote the scriptures. He worked in Rumi to make the verses of unity-in-love. There were golden illuminated Qurans. An ingeniously carved lectern (rahle) for reading cross-legged. It had survived well, for it wouldn't have borne someone sitting on it. There were woolen felt caps belonging to Rumi. I wonder if he wore them?

Outside the tomb they met an Imam from Paris. Phim said, We're learning about Islam. Please teach us a hadith to treasure. The Imam said, A controversial hadith, collected by Qadi Iyad (1083-1149), the teacher of Averroes (1126-1198): Iyad reported that Muhammad responded to a question by Ali about faith with seventeen principles. Let us consider the first five. Knowledge is my capital. Intellect my basis of faith. Love is my foundation. Longing is my vessel. Remembrance of God is my comfort. Note how in these five golden sayings of Muhammad the mind is in pursuit of God.

(With thanks to Kabir Helminski's reflection on Muhammad's Sunnah.)

The Imam continued. Each principle requires exposition. Let's consider number seven, "Sorrow is my companion." Sorrow is a rare word in the Quran. What does Muhammad mean? Sorrow is a virtue, as it was in ancient days: solemnity, sadness, dignity. Gaiety and laughter were the stuff of fools. The good teacher feels sorrow because humanity suffers. Remember the poor, the sick, the captives. How about number ten? "Contentment is a blessing." Phim said, I've heard that before. The Imam said, If only the people of faith could share truth and enact our love more fully.

(This is called the Hadith of Muhammad's Sunnah)

153   Felting

They were visiting the Folkcraft Centre. Felting takes us back to our Altai mountain roots, said the guide. Sheep and goats, a heap of wool, water and pressure. Lo, a sturdy tent wall or a rug. Mehmet, a living national treasure, showed them. He laid out a large rectangle with a floral patterns in orange, red, blue and indigo pieces. A thick layer of fluffy white wool. Sprinkled water. Rolled in a carpet. Bound up by cord. Placed in a press. He rolled it out. A beautiful felt rug. The flowers glowed. Phim felt it, soft and warm. How much?

(Mastercraftsman Mehmet Girgiç in Konya. He makes the dervish felt hats sikke.)

The guide said, This village preserved the Cappadocian Greek language until 1923, when the population exchanges took place. They'd lived in peaceful co-existence. Rumi (it is said) had witnessed a miracle at the Orthodox monastery of Saint Chariton (now called Akmanastir). He built a small mosque there, and required the Turks to protect the Greek villagers, allowing them the honor to clean his tomb. They preserved their language and faith for 800 years. They're now in Nea Silata village, Halkidiki. Konya had been in Seljuk hands since c. 1100. Rumi appeared a hundred years later with his holy truths.

(Sille Subaşı Village NW of Konya. St Helena Church. Aya Elena)

Phim yelled as the cafe latte, still piping hot, seeped through his trousers. Ow! Ow! Ow! He grabbed the cup but it was already empty. He jumped up and danced about. Water! Sal thinking quickly, sloshed his ice-cold Coca Cola, and Phim cried, Thanks! Irma said, Clumsy fool. Phim said, I was jogged. Yaeli said, That guy there. A man in a pinstripe suit hurried out of the cafe. He glanced at Phim. His mouth twisted. The waiter brought towels. Joseph said, We need to find a laundry. A friendly Turk said, Near the souk. Coins.

The laundromat started leaking, water flooded out of the bottom, from underneath. In a short time it was a stream of soap suds. They got onto the benches. Phim was panicking. Sal, how are we going to stop this? Sal said, Water supply. Sudan said, It's increasing. Phim took his shoes and socks off, and stepped down. Ow! It was extremely hot. He hopped back onto the bench. A crowd gathered outside the laundry, murmuring. The hot soapy stream flowed into the gutter. Jumping from bench to chair, Irma and Yaeli got to the door and cried, Help!

A huge burly Turk with a beard and bald head strode towards them. What's the problem? Ah! He stepped boldly forward, found the main tap, and turned it off; he went to the offending machine, and thumped it hard. It coughed and fell silent. This is the wrong place, he said. It is out of order. Come to Derva Laundry. They gathered up Phim's soapy clothes (he was wearing red stripy pajamas) and went to the new place. The crowd outside were amused at Phim, and laughed. He felt scalded and peeved but tried not to show it.

The Imam explained. The Ottomans were often very pious, though it varied from Sultan to Sultan. Five Holy Nights, called Kandil, were established for pious celebration of the life of Muhammad from the sixteenth century. His birth, his conception, his miraj (heaven journey), forgiveness of sins, and the first revelation of the Quran by Gabriel. We form a circle of faithful around the Imam, and chant deep resonant prayers, calling upon God and praising him. Phim asked, Is it possible to attend? The Imam said, Normally it is Muslims only, but I will make an exception for you.

The Imam continued. We are celebrating the revelation of the Quran, Laylat-al-Qadr, the Night of Power, Kadir Gecesi in Turkish. The revelation started in 610 CE in the Hira cave on Mount Jabal al-Nour in Mecca. Come with me. We have a special gallery and you and your friends can witness our prayer service. The Imam knelt in the centre of a large circle of men about sixty strong, many with green turbans wound with white sashes, white shirts and black trousers. They knelt likewise facing in towards the Imam, who glanced up briefly at Phim.

The Imam begin with prayers and then chanted Bismillah. The men joined in, and the Mosque echoed with their solemn voices. They stood and chanted. Deep rumbling booming voices like a wall of strength. Praise be to God (Allah), the creator of all created, who sustains life, who lifts the dawn, all-glorious God. Power surged outwards from them. Their love for God and wish to give all their hope to him, that all be safe and good for the family. Suddenly Phim saw them as a galaxy of stars wheeling through space chanting in joy.

The Imam explained later. The night of power is mentioned in the five verse Surah Al-Qadr (97). It is considered to have special virtue. It is better than a thousand months. With the permission of the Lord, the angels and the Spirit (Ruh, who is Gabriel) descend to earth to carry out their duty. The night of power is filled with peace until dawn. Muhammad's wife, Aisha, asked him for a prayer to say, and he said, "My God! You are forgiving. You are generous. Your nature is mercy. Grant me forgiveness also. Amen."

Phim read, The finest example of Seljuk architecture, built 1251 by Celaluddin Karatay, Emir of Konya, servant of the Sultan, friend of Rumi. The painstaking attention to beauty proclaimed the piety. It was originally a seminary, now a tile museum. The monumental door is impressive. A large rectangular wall frames a Romanesque arch which holds a square doorway. The upper half is decorated with blue and white stone with parallel interconnecting lines. Muqarnas in the arch above the door. Running above and midway there are friezes of holy verses. For knowledge of heaven and earth, enter here.

The tile work in the dome was astonishing. There were blue, turquoise and white lines forming twenty four pointed stars in a complex mathematical tessellation. Phim gazed in wonder at the patience and ingenuity they must have shown. It was obviously a pictorial representation of a starry sky. In the centre of the dome there was a skylight which was a turret with windows around and wooden roof. Some of the tiles had been lost. On the arches there were tiles with script. On the walls a different pattern. On completion it must have been the pride of Konya.

There were fragments of the original decorations. Plaster with floral patterns. Most interesting were the painted tiles showing influence from the Far East. Hooded and hatted nobles from a pre-Islamic era. Look at that, a symbolic sun, perhaps a memory of ancient Seljuk faith. A long-haired noble sat cross-legged drinking wine. An eagle seized a lamb. An archer. A blue heron with thin legs and long beak. A bird with a human face. This is the best one, said Irma. A horse galloped joyfully. The tiles come from the Kubadabad Palace excavation, read Phim.

(Kubadabad Palace summer residence of Sultan Alaaddin Keykubad, Lake Beysehir)

Look, said Phim, the pattern above the main door is like the Karatay. The same interlaced blue and white stone strap forming a circle above the arch. Surely it's a message. In the Karatay there were three bosses, like stars. Here, just the circle.   Perfection, said Sal. God above the arch.   It could be the sun, said Sudan.   A diagram of the heavenly realm, said Joseph. Remember the sky was holy to the ancient Turks.   Inside the mosque there was a forest of reused columns. A well preserved Corinthian capital with curling leaf. Yaeli said, Ancient Roman or Greek?

Sal said, Look at this fine workmanship. The minbar was carved in dark polished walnut, imitating the best stone carving and done with precision so that each Arabic letter could be clearly made out, a line of script running joyfully over the pointed arch. Above this there were three interconnected six-pointed stars. Orion? Stairs led up to the pulpit. The imam stood here, admonishing the Seljuks, who were becoming affluent. Islam's strength was its classless embrace of the people. Sultan and lowly slave, bow in equality before God. God is one and we are one in God.

The guide explained. This was the high point of the ancient city. There was an acropolis and pagan temples. They must have been all demolished by the Christians. Konya was a strong Christian centre, as indicated by the mention in Acts 14 (Iconium). Later, when it became the Seljuk capital, all the churches became mosques. With the cult of Rumi and his teaching, the city became a holy pilgrimage site. Here's the mihrab. Beautiful turquoise tiles ran the Baqara surah around the alcove, which was sculpted in stone. Phim stood before it, filling his mind with a prayer to God.

Gerrruu Geru Geru cooed the turtle dove, sounding for some reason like a frog. Sitting in the Kültürpark in Konya, with a book of Sufi poetry, Jelal the teacher (originally a Quaker from Pennsylvania) was with them. Jelal said, Phim, The dove was greatly beloved by the Ottomans. I came to the Mevlana Sufi path when I met an old master here, the last survivor from the Ottoman era. He was a collared dove in grey plumage. The Master Rumi has the iridescent rainbow of a wood pigeon. How beautiful the eye and beak of the dove.

Jelal was teaching Rumi. A favourite ghazal. The moment that you are with yourself, you are under the clouds of sorrow; and the moment you are selfless, the moon will come to your side. The moment that you are with yourself, your beloved will depart from you; and the moment you are selfless, you will taste the beloved's wine. The moment that you are with yourself, you will feel the chill of November; and the moment that you are selfless, winter will blossom like spring.   The beloved is Allah. "Yourself" is your selfish ego; to be "selfless" is the goal.

(Inspired by interview with Kabir Helminski about Sufism. Poem found in *Love's Ripening: Rumi on the Heart's Journey*. Trans. By Kabir Helminski & Ahmad Rezwami.)

What is a true Sufi today, said Jelal.
We're at a critical point in world history.
We cannot have war. We need unity in
human   government.   Forces   work
against peace. We must look for the best
in each other. We must see the values of
different cultures and different religions,
even different sects in our own faith.
Diversity is a treasure given by God. It is
part of the plan. No religion has a
monopoly on truth. We should love our
own tradition. It is our gift. Be grateful
for it. There are many wavelengths in a
prism of light.

(Inspired by interview with Kabir Helminski about Sufism.)

171 Love Is

Jelal said, Consider these verses. I'll explain in a moment: Dawn is the decree of the sun. Love of God, the Sultan's monogram. The time of union has come now. Love is interpreted this way. Look at the One. The compassion of the universe. Look at how He uplifts the poor. Mantles are as bright as the moon. Shawls smell like roses. Love is the whole thing. We are only pawns. Love is a sea without shore. We are a drop in it. He brings forth hundreds of proofs. They are our surest guide. The sky turns only with Love.

(Lines adapted from Verse 1 in *Divan-i-Kebir*, trans. by Nevit Oguz Ergin.)

Jelal explained: Dawn commands us to rise, to live, to love. Monogram is the seal, the name. Union is the feeling of God's presence; happiness; also unity in passion. God is mercy. He grants knowledge of himself to the poor and allows them happiness in their lives. "Rose" a symbol of God, his presence, joy, exaltation. The identity of God, his way of working is "love," both the highest spiritual form and all forms. "Proof" is the Islamic idea that the created world is a sure proof or guide that God exists, and He is love.

(The monogram is the Ottoman tughra, a calligraphic emblem of authority.)

173   Full Moon

Jelal said: The full moon is inside your house. But my friends and I run into the street. I'm in here, he calls. We aren't listening. We're looking up at the sky. In the garden the nightingale sobs. We coo like ringdoves. Where? Where? Lo, I am with you. God is in the thought of searching. Nearer to you than yourself. There's no need to go outside. Wash yourself of yourself. Be melting snow. A white flower grows in the quietness. Let your tongue become that flower.

(Adapted from Ghazal 2172 from *Diwan-e Shams*, versions by Coleman Barks, Kabir Edmund Helminski, Peter Lamborn Wilson, Nasrullah Pourjavadi.)

Jelal said: Even if your beloved is a pool of fire jump in. Keep burning. On the night of separation keep burning. Burn like a candle and melt. Don't think hostility. Build peace. If they rip your clothes to shreds, just keep on weaving unity. A Sema appears in the work of peace. Listen to the pipe and tambourine. Will the musicians crumble into chaos? Be a million in yourself. One bright candle burning peace. Separation was absence from God; unity with God was the goal.

(Adapted from *Divan-i-Kebir*, trans. by Nevit Oguz Ergin.)

175   Wine

Jelal said: O Beautiful, offer wine. Cure the drunkenness of the drunks with the love that is reflected in your face. Bring the aged wine. Serve at early dawn so roses will be scattered around. Even the sky becomes exuberant because of the wine of drunks. Jelal explained: It's puzzling. Beautiful must be God. Wine must be spiritual inspiration. Drunk must be the state of elevated joy and hope. Rose is unity with God. The feeling is that God is here! The sky at dawn the color of drunken faces, rosy-red. A cup of heavenly aged wine.

(Adapted from *Divan-i-Kebir,* trans. by Nevit Oguz Ergin.)

Jelal told a story from Masnavi: Ayaz, the favorite officer of Sultan Mahmud of Ghazna, was accused of going each morning to a secret chamber and worshipping hidden treasure. His enemies reported this. The Sultan sent a spy. They discovered that he kept in the room a pair of old shoes and a tatty coat. They were to remind him of when he had been destitute, to make him grateful each day for the bounty of the Sultan. Ayaz said, "Who knows himself truly, knows his Lord."

(*Masnavi* Book 5 story 8. Adapted from Annemarie Schimmel, *Rumi's World.*)

Jelal explained: Nafs is a key concept in the Quran, and in Sufi teaching. In the Quran it means self, or soul, with the idea of free will. For the Sufi, spiritual advance requires mastery of the nafs. At first, the nafs prompts towards evil, like an unruly donkey. Rumi compares it to a camel that must be turned towards the dwelling of the beloved. In the second stage of spiritual growth, the conscience awakens. One tries to be good. In the third stage the nafs is at peace, accepting nothing but the will of God.

Jelal was explaining: The poet uses the image of his own heart throughout his poetry. "His love seized my heart and smelled it; if it were not good, would it smell sweet?" A house, a garden, a mosque, a fish in a frying pan, a window. The heart was also a mirror that needed to be polished, to reflect the face of the beloved. Or it was a house that had to be swept by the broom of "Lā," the first word of the Shahada, the profession of Islamic faith. Nothing but God. Only the beloved. "Lā ilāha illa'llāh!"

(Adapted from Annemarie Schimmel, *Rumi's World*. Dil: heart.)

179 Grilled

Jelal said: A man knocked at the door. His beloved asked, "Who are You?" He said, "It's me." He answered, "Go away! No place here for the raw." He went away, and separation grilled him with a fierce flame. He crackled, crisped and curled. He was done to a turn. He matured. He approached the door, and raised his hand. His beloved called out, "Who's there?" He replied, "You are here. It is you at the door." The beloved said, "Come in. Now you're me. There's no room in this house for two 'I's."

(Adapted from Annemarie Schimmel, *Rumi's World. Mathnavi* 1.3056-63.)

Jelal sang a few verses: Listen to the reed. How I am yearning. I lament my separation. Ever since I was taken from the reed bed, I've wept with longing to return. I am far from my roots. Let me go back to my home. Let me grow a heart to feel it. Let my song break into fire. I am not wind. I am fire. I am the thought of my beloved. I am drunk. I am madness. I am nothing more than I am, filled with the song of my love.

(Freely adapted from the beginning of *Mathnavi* 1.1-18. With thanks to Franklin Lewis & Ibrahim Gamard.)

As Phim was listening to Jelal talk about Rumi, a memory broke through of walking along the Cornish coastal path. It was a sunny day with his mother. The sea sparkled. There was a pleasant breeze. The heather was in blossom. Mum said, Sea horses! They sat together. She looked happy, relaxed. She sang, "Little fishes swimming in the mighty tide." Phim loved her voice. Why didn't she sing more? "Mackerel and herring, the fishermen cried." Choughs performed acrobatics above the cliff. Were they playing with the wind? Phim peered through his bins. How surprising. Their legs were scarlet.

Jelal sang one of his own songs: All my desire is this. A grain of wheat in its husk. Let the wind help me. A sack of dry grain. Let the river flow onward. We are thankful, lord. You granted us grain. Milled under stone. We have fine white flour. Knead the dough in the cool morning. Is there fuel for the oven? Dried palms and dried dung. A pile of flat loaves. Sprinkle with salt. We go to the prayer. Life in the grain, in milling and baking, in the round loaves, we offer to God.

(Inspired by "The Mill, the Stone, and the Water," by Robert Bly. *The Rumi Collection*. Ed Kabir Helminski.).

183   Milling

Jelal said: The gift of insight. When the barriers are removed, the eye penetrates to read the tablet of the unseen, looking to the origin, hearing the quarrel between the angels of earth and the Divine Majesty. They do not recognize father Adam as God's steward (is this who I am, thought Phim, or who we all are?) Insight goes to the root of the root; to the Day of Decision (Quran 77.14; 78.17). In life's milling, phrases fled within his mind, his understanding perished repeatedly. What was the point? Phim tried again and fought to hold the insight.

(Adapted from "Heroes," from *Mathnawi* 4.2881 and following. Trans. Kabir Helminski,
The Rumi Collection, ed. Kabir Helminski.)

Phim, said Jelal, start with basics. The practice of dhikr. Remember God with every breath. You've been in Maaloula? I've been in Iraq. I've chanted with Christian and Jew, using the holy name Allah. Allah gathers all names; it is a blessed sound. Breathe in. Breathe out. As you breathe out, utter the Arabic pronoun "he" which refers to God, "hu." Jelal breathed out, "huuu" a breath of peace. Join me as I sing Allah. Jelal lifted a drum. His fingers sounded a heartbeat, chanting Allah Allah Allah. Phim sang too, then Irma'am, Yaeli, Saleem, Sudan and Joseph.

Later, Phim was reading about Rumi. "They called the rain rahmet mercy, like the Prophet, mercy to the world. Spring brought the marriage of heaven and earth, an allegory. 'You are my sky; I'm the earth.' He would listen to the water mill, its voice longing for home (heaven). The soft breeze on the hillside was also mercy nafas ar-rahman 'breath of the merciful.' Touched by the breeze, the branches became drunk and joined the dance of Creation. They clapped their hands and stamped their feet, repeating the first dance, when God said, Am I not your Lord?"

(Sura 21.107; Sura 7.172. Adapted from Annemarie Schimmel, *Rumi's World*.)

Phim was reading about Rumi. "When you gaze on the plants and roses you will read the message of eternity. The spring breeze becomes visible. It required the earth's nutrition, and rain from above. From within us our souls must become visible in action; in the same way the Spirit is made visible. Every leaf is a messenger, crying out with green tongues of the miraculous power of God." Phim looked at the garden. He feasted his eyes on a peony. A chaffinch was singing from the tree.

(Adapted from Schimmel, *Rumi's World*. Cp. G. M. Hopkins' "Pied Beauty;" John Keats' "Ode to Melancholy.")

Phim was listening to a Sufi Song. "Listen, dear one. My voice is within you. I've called you often. You do not hear me. I am the will between the seen and the unseen.   Through me you find yourself. Why do you flee me? Others love you to take you, not for whom you are. Love me only. Love yourself in me. I am the fragrance in every fragrance. I am the savor in every savor. You have not smelled me or tasted me yet." It was a solemn Spanish-Arab dance, a guitar strumming.

(Adapted from Ibn Arabi, "Sufi Song." See "The Threshold Society" website.)

188   Pen

Phim was writing a Rumi poem. "I am a pen in my beloved's hand. I write alif, lam. He trims me and dips me. On the parchment I sing of my love. How well we get on together. Smoothly the paper receives my blood black scritching. I talk of bowing my head in joy, of finding his name. The ink is my soul. Am I reluctant? Fill me again. Let me write. I lie idle, dry and empty. Where have you gone? I am lost without you. Let me walk towards you. O my beloved, let me live."

(Freely adapted with additions, from version by Annemarie Schimmel, *Rumi's World*. Verse 2530 *Divan i Shams*.)

Phim listened to a clip of pop music, the singer quoting from Rumi. Her voice was gentle and soothing. The oud was entrancing. There were women singing peacefully in the background. She sang, "I saw myself as the source of existence. I was there in the beginning. I was the spirit of love. Now I am sober, there is only the hangover. The memory." Had she gone mad? In her rapture had she dreamed herself at one with God; and now it was over, she felt exhausted and bereaved? Then she said, "Roses! I too have been covered with thorns."

(Inspired by song by M. L. Ciccone (1958-   ))

Jelal said, We live in an age of tourism. We live in peace and learn to love one another. We can visit holy places. But we should preserve respect for sacred life, whatever the house we visit. This whirling dervish dance is holy. It is offered to God to bring blessings. The dancers are brothers who have walked a path of sacrifice and love. They have suffered, passing through stages in order to be worthy to give you this gift. It is for all who seek. Open the eyes of spirit, and be ready to feel that God is here.

Jelal said, Rumi was a scholar of the Quran. He was moist clay. He was fired in God's kiln. He found the inner secret of love. It was a madness granted by heaven. Love burns us up. It is needed to make us fully human. We are an incomplete evolution. Love completes us. The loss of the "ego" is the step required. To be empty of ego. To be filled with the consciousness of God's light and God's truth, the feeling of the total goodness and love of God, alive in his laws, his words and his prophet Muhammad.

(Inspired by Sunnah Muakadah "Rumi Documentary." https://youtu.be/Cf1c2-L0DmU)

Jelal said, True spiritual nature yearns to be reunited with God; as the reed in the ney yearns to be reunited with the reed bed. Lamenting to return to the holy origin. The reed flute can only make a sound with the breath blown into it. It is like Adam, alive by virtue of the breath of God. When the human being is perfect, then the breath through their existence will sound like God, because their "ego" is absent, and only God's breath is there. Jesus was like this when he spoke. Listen to Jesus, the wisdom of God.

(Inspired by Sunnah Muakadah "Rumi Documentary." https://youtu.be/Cf1c2-L0DmU)

Jelal said, The Mevlevi truth was not revealed in the West. Why not? Because it's no different to the highest truth perceived by the Jews and the Christians. Look at the arms crossed on the chest. Letter, sign, unity. Once you have grasped this and felt it to the core of your being, how could you be anyone's enemy? How could you submit to the political and military wickedness of past ages? You become mad to the world; and sane before God. Sanity is total love, but the human race is still far from this. Selfish, basic, greedy human race.

Jelal explained the dance. The dancer rejects the ego and the world, and rises to God. The tall felt hat is a tombstone. The white skirts are a shroud. The black cloak is the world (daily concerns). He casts off his cloak. Silently chanting God's name in his mind, the dancer revolves anticlockwise, balancing on his left foot, his right foot turning. The dust on the inner mirror is wiped clean to allow God to shine. The right arm is lifted to heaven; the left arm to earth, transmitting blessings. Look, they become planets whirling for love of God.

They were attending the Sema. In her mind, Irma'am was dancing with them. She was a dervish, dancing on a moonlit platform under cloudless skies. As she whirled, the stars above her made circles. She felt sublimely happy. The music was heavenly. She sang out in Coptic a holy phrase. Round and round, thanking God, her mind filling with brightness until there came a feeling of holy presence, and sudden fear and joy mingled all together, and she paused, looking around. The dance continued. There was Phim, enrapt, enjoying the music.

As they drove away from Konya, a dark cloud descended on Phim. History was a nightmare of injustice to him once again; he lay in the road; an endless stream of sorrow walked through his mind. Tell our story, what they did to us Phim, their clever selfish cruelty. He lay under the tracks of a thousand locomotives, hammering through. O O O it was true, brother, sister, Africa, Asia, First Nation children: the world was not fair or good. Weary with grief, help me God he cried.

197   Demiryolu Geçidi

Sal stopped before the white St Andrew's cross. They'd come to a level crossing. The red-white bar was down. Red lights flashing. Bong bong bong.   Phim looked out the window.   How many of these in Turkey?   What's that?   Up the tracks, on the right, a young woman with baby. She looked around. She lay down holding the baby. Without thinking, Phim leapt out of the car, shouting, No! No!   He dodged under the bar and went to the woman. She resisted. Her face riven with suffering. Sound of train approaching. Phim looked up. It was upon them.

(Demiryolu Geçidi: Level Crossing)

Phim grabbed her and hit the ground, pulling her and the baby down. Allah, he cried, the train passed over them, a mighty wind, and he felt an edge touch the back of his head, and pushed himself and the woman close to the dirt. It seemed to last forever. The slightest move upward and he was dead. Knowing that he was miraculously alive, he sang out in his heart a phrase he remembered from school long ago: Whereof we rejoice. He felt the woman move and held her still. It was over. Quick to the car.

("Whereof we rejoice" from "Song of Freedom" Ps 126 in *Bible Songs* by C.V. Stanford.)

199   Harem Ballet

Ankara State Ballet were performing in the ancient Roman Theatre at Aspendos. It was a warm still evening. They each rented a large cushion. Padishah (the sultan) was dancing with Gulbeden, his beloved. His powerful mother opposed the match. Gulbeden wore a crimson dress. He wore shimmering green silk with a gold cummerbund. Round and round she span in his hands; he stood back, his arms thrown up in joy. What exultation! On his knees before her; then he lifted her high. He turned her face toward him. How bewitching thou art!

(Turkish ballet "Harem" choreographed & written by Merih Çimenciler 1998.)

The spotlight followed a ballerina who performed a short piece. The orchestra played a lively folk dance. She wore a knee-length white frilly dress which blossomed outwards as she span. There was a red rose pinned at her heart. She was exceptionally light on her feet, bright and exuberant, turning here and there, attentive and curious, delighted to be the best.   How confident she is, thought Phim.   What a spirit of joy, whispered Yaeli to Irma.   The audience was quiet in admiration. The ballerina turned the whole world about her as she danced.

(Inspired by Ayşem Sunal Savaşkurt dancing "La Fille Mal Gardée" chor. Joseph Lazzini.)

There was an ice cream vendor. Let's get an ice cream, said Phim. What have you got? Dondurma, said the man with a smile. He was wearing a red spangly waistcoat and a fez. How do you make Dondurma, asked Phim. Goat's milk, salep, mastic (resin), sugar, all churned together. Delicious Turkish ice cream! He scooped up a cone-full, handed it to Phim who took it, whereupon he whipped it away, Phim tried to grab it, failed to, he returned it, snatched it away again, dabbed Phim's nose, and gave it to him with a smile.

(Salep: flour from tubers of Orchis mascula & militaris. Ancient Roman aphrodisiac.)

Sal looked up and counted.   Octagonal, he said.   A harmonious red brick tower. Begun in 1230 when the Seljuks took the city, and finished 1373. Inside the mosque were ancient columns and Roman pipes beneath the floor. There was an imam.   Can we ascend the minaret?   No, he said.   Phim told him about their journey, and he softened. They climbed up 90 steps (38 m). The view was splendid. The old city with red roofs and the dark-brown tiles of the mosque. Daglari mountains stood in the west. The city spread over the plain, the blue Med shining.

(Yivli Minare Fluted Minaret Kaleiçi, Antalya.)

The broken minaret had been repaired. It was a tall round tower on an hexagonal base, with cone turret. A sister to the fluted minaret. The mosque had been a Roman temple, Christian church (Panagia Virgin Mary), mosque again, then church, and again mosque. They'd just finished restoring it. Marble pillars banded with steel; ancient Roman decorative borders. Rebuilt arches. New roof. Look at these photos, Phim, said Sal. It'd been a complete ruin. The restoration showed each historical period. It was now a house of prayer again. Irma said, If only Christian and Muslim could share these ancient sanctuaries.

(Şehzade Korkut Mosque, Kaleiçi restoration completed January 2022.)

Phim gazed on the statue in astonishment. The body turned in the dance, the thin chiton clinging to her like a veil of water, revealing her breasts and curves, accentuating the erotic appeal. She was plump; obviously young, rich and healthy; a face like Athena; the viewers were meant to see her and delight, both men and women — what did it mean? Marriage, fertility, joy. The folds and shape of the garment are like a flow of water caught in the air. A naiad dancing in rapture? Phim glanced at Irma, who seemed to be sharing his amazement.

(Antalya Archaeol. Museum, Dancing Woman from Perge c. 200 CE [Hellenistic copy]; cp Nereid Monument, from Xanthos c. 380 BCE, British Museum.)

The beaches were white sand and the water turquoise blue. There was a group attempting the world depth record for free diving. A woman in a red wetsuit plunged down to 70 m. Phim and the others watched from shore. She held her breath about two minutes. She rose like a cork and took rapid shallow breaths. On shore she was interviewed by a TV channel. She spoke to Sudan. I came here to protest at ecological damage. Look at how much litter there is! I'd like to start straightaway. She bent down and picked up a plastic tube.

(Lake Salda, Yeşilova, Burdur.)

Sabriye, the diver, said, Let's walk around the lake. They walked on the sand. It was an idyllic day of perfect sunshine. She said, This lake is utterly unique. It's exceptionally deep. It has unusual minerals. The hills around are still wooded. We have wildlife surviving, but tourism has had such a negative impact. Can you feel the breeze coming to us from over the water? Isn't it holy? Allah is calling us to love and defend the beauty of the world.   Irma said, I hear it as well.   Sudan said, It is a certain call to our generation.

All of a sudden a strong man stood in front of Phim. He had a snarling twisted expression. Wearing a mitre-fez with a lira ₺ sign encircled with barbed wire. You've gotta choice. Give up now and come to my knife, or struggle, and I will slice bits off you to have some fun. He put his knife to Phim's throat. Holding Phim, he inserted the razor-sharp tip into Phim's rib cage and sliced through shirt and flesh. Phim gave an almighty yell. Sabriye paused an instant and threw herself at the man, punching him hard between the eyes.

The man staggered, still holding Phim. Sabriye was quick. She hit him again. Her fist struck his head like a hammer. He went down. Phim got up, holding his side, bleeding into his white shirt. Sabriye watched the man, who was getting up. As he rose, she struck him again. He went out like a light. Sal said, You are extremely good. Sabriye laughed. Ancestors were Balkan Janissaries. We were fierce. Family in the police force. Joseph said, Thank you for saving him. Can you help us find a clinic? It wasn't deep, and a couple of stitches were enough.

The church (520) was built on an earlier church, honoring Saint Nicholas' relics. He'd been Bishop of Myra and present at the Council of Nicaea (325). They now held liturgies on Dec 6. The original floor was level polished stone (opus sectile) with hexagonal tiles of expensive marble. Sections were marked out for analogions. There was an intriguing pattern of four circles around a large circle. The four Gospels? suggested Irma. Beside it, two interlaced squares making a star holding a sphere. In between, a beautiful sphere with light-blue triangular mosaics. The design was held in a rectangular frame.

(Demre. Restored Byzantine Church. Saint Nicholas of Myra 270-343.)

Sudan said, It's a miracle there are any left. The guide said, We've established a breeding program, gathering eggs and hatching them ourselves and releasing them safely to the sea. We share data and expertise with sister projects in Greece and Israel.   Peace in action, said Irma.   Schools are involved, said the guide, they learn about the sea turtle, the marine environment. We maintain a map of the Mediterranean showing how many clutches are laid, and we track turtles electronically. Sudan said, The more you can teach the better. If you can save the turtle, you'll save the Mediterranean.

(Kaplumbağa Loggerhead sea turtle Caretta caretta Izutuzu Beach; in honour of June Haimoff MBE.)

Phim remembered the Mock Turtle passage in *Alice in Wonderland*. Was Carroll teaching a lesson? Turtle soup had been a fashionable delicacy in London (18th century). Green Turtles were hunted to near-extinction. On land, tears flow from their lachrymal glands, which remove excess salt. He viewed a clip of a loggerhead. Large eloquent eyes and grim determined mouth. They rowed gracefully through the blue depths. They were an ancient dinosaur survivor, traversing the world's oceans. They existed millions of years before Adam stood up and walked. Where was it they had creation myths about the great Sea Turtle?

(Lewis Carroll, *Alice in Wonderland* 1865.)

Yaeli was driving. It was a beautiful valley, with the narrow road cut into the steep hillside above the river. There were wooded slopes and rocky outcrops. The Merc was running smoothly. Yaeli was singing in Hebrew. Irma was listening in admiration. She was so talented. What are you singing, Yaeli? Psalm 117. It's a Yemeni melody I learnt. In the synagogue we sing the prayers in various styles. Phim heard Hallelujah. That sounds so good when you sing it, he said. Hallelu, said Yaeli, originally meant shine, and then changed to praise.

The road was narrow. The Merc filled the right-hand lane, the front left wheel ran close to the centre-line. The right wheels by the low stone wall that boarded the road. The river far below. Yaeli noticed that the car crept over the centre-line, though she was holding it steady.   Ange, something's strange. We keep moving into the other lane.   A truck hurtled by, going too fast. It was close. The wheel became stiff. Yaeli fought for control.   Ange said, Stop the car if you can. A car appeared. It was going to be a head-on.

Phim reached from behind and turned the wheel with Yaeli, and the Merc swerved aside, scraping the stone wall, but avoiding the crash. There was nowhere to stop. Ange and Sal were now on full alert, but there was little to be done until they could stop. Yaeli slowed down, fighting the steering wheel, which was possessed by a force turning the wheels left. Phim and Irma joined hands and reached forward, both touching Yaeli.   Irma sang, Halleluia, Mary! Phim sang Amen.   Yaeli said, I've got control again. They pulled over in a lay-by.

They stopped by an ancient humpback stone bridge. The arches were hemispheres. As they walked along the river, they saw the bridge reflected on the surface, making three perfect circles. Phim waded under the bridge. It was quite shallow. The flow was swift. The water was silty, a light brown. The Meander laughed and chortled, rushing over a small step, and hurried smoothly on. Phim looked in the water, and saw a wavering reflection. He looked closer and toppled in. Phim! cried Sal, your Turkish baptism, laughing. Tastes quite good, if a bit riverish, said Phim.

(Hançalar Bridge on the Meander River, Denizli, Çal.)

Joseph said, The Meander river was celebrated by the Greeks and is often mentioned.   Sudan said, The fertile valley must have been a prize possession. Isn't there something in the name, asked Phim. The first part Maia and second part Andros. The universal Mother was a cult figure in this region, bearing different names. Is it "Maia-husband" or "Maia-man?" It used to flood. A powerful god. Like the Nile? They spoke of it "turning back upon itself" and "hiding the direction it flowed."   Sal said, There's some ancient pre-Greek veneration. Is it a life-giving creator serpent?

(Meander River Μαιανδρος Maiandros in Greek; quotations by Ovid and Propertius.)

The North Theatre was covered in grass. A green amphitheater. You could imagine it being used for teaching, said Irma. Joseph said, The Greeks sent Jewish families here, who became rich, sending gold to the Temple each year. It was famous for wealth, cloth production and eye ointment. Phim said, Jews and Greeks building prosperity, probably intermarrying. They would favor the Christian message. Joseph said, The angel is critical of their tepid faith, "because you are lukewarm, and neither cold nor hot, I am about to spit you out of my mouth." Irma said, Jesus once spat on the earth.

(Mk 6.39-40; Mk 8.22-26; John 9.6-7; Revelation 3.14-18; about the Jews, see Cicero 'Pro Flaccus.')

They rose early and got to the entrance at 06:30 when it opened. The sun was up but the snowy slopes were still in shadow. There were few people about. It had been a place of wonder to ancient peoples. The calcium-rich thermal water welled from the mountain and flowed into steaming turquoise pools. As they walked by, the sun rose higher and shone upon them, sending their shadows long-legged and long-armed onto the white surface. Yaeli struck poses and said, What letter is this?   X Chi (kaɪ), said Phim and   Yaeli said, א Alef, fool.

The ancient baths had been restored and were now the museum. The guide said, Regard the huge barrel vault. The baths were once a Basilica. Christian architecture adopted the arch and vaulting of the great public baths and the Colosseum, even though they abhorred both institutions, and banned them. Later they used columns from temples. Irma said, Look, three priestesses. One with a cornucopia, the central one holding a statue of Cybele, one leading a sacrificial heifer, pouring water upon it. The cornucopia priestess had her robes tucked up, standing in the healing waters. Plentiful harvest in their crowns.

(Denizli Hierapolis (Pamukkale) Archaeological Museum.)

The guide showed them the Plutonion. They've excavated the cave entrance, blocked up by the Christians in the fourth century. There's a seismic fault, and an upwelling spring, with sulphuric and carbonic gases released. They thought it was the gate to Hades, guarded by Pluto. They threw in sacrificial animals which were killed, and dragged them out with ropes. Strabo comments on it killing sparrows. It was a place of fear and wonder. People would come and ask for an oracle and pay a large fee. Perhaps they were also propitiating Pluto. Many people came to Hierapolis seeking a cure.

There was a concert that evening in the restored theatre. You could rent a cushion. The audience was limited to 5,000. Sound engineers and architects had rebuilt the theatre wall and placed a sounding wall of fibreglass to reflect sound. Sitting on the platform in the centre was a man with a bağlama. The acoustic was perfect. It was a folksong, an allegory of the struggles of modern Turkey. Raising the people to better life. Better education, better health. "Gidiyorum gündüz gece." Phim's neighbour translated. "I walk day and night." Soon all the Turks were singing, and Phim joined in.

(Aşık Veysel 1894-1973 folk artist & poet "Uzun İnce Bir Yoldayım." I walk a long narrow road.)

They were looking at the columnar statue of Aphrodite, who was worshipped at Afrodisias. Perhaps Epaphras was a convert from her cult. She was encased in a tunic adorned with four levels of imagery. Under her tunic she wore a full-length chiton. On the tunic could be seen the three Graces; a married pair, said to be Gaia and Uranos, Earth and Heaven; Helios (sun) and Selene (moon); marine Aphrodite riding a sea-goat; and a group of Erotes (Cupids) performing rituals. Joseph said, Greek Aphrodite is united with an ancient local mother goddess with cosmic powers.

(Afrodisias Museum; Epaphras Col 1.7; Col 4.12-13; Epaphroditus Php 2.25-30.)

In the park there was a woman in white with a long red shawl wrapped around her head, with a box of local figs. She showed them to Phim, each mauve-brown fruit with a veil of white yeast. Small globular shining fruits. She opened one and showed the brilliant ruby. She smiled at Phim. Who were your ancestors, thought Phim. Irma, let's get some. How much? Cheap, the woman said in Turkish. She washed them in alcohol and they ate one each. Sweet succulent figs. I could eat a dozen, said Phim. Greed, said Yaeli.

The woman said, Come with me to our orchard on the hillside. They followed the van into the Aydin hills.   I will show you how to pick figs. You reach up and twist.   Phim did so, and the fig came away, oozing white sticky sap.   Very good, she said, large lustrous eyes. Phim said, What do figs mean in Turkish poetry?   Irma said, Phim, don't ask strange questions.   Yaeli said, Same as the Bible.   The woman said, You may think one thing; I may think another; but the truth is here, look, this beauty, here, and she opened one again.

The woman said, Let's make fig jam,
adding white sugar and water to a kilo
of figs, and simmering.   Phim, she said,
Skim off the foam.   It turned dark,
filling the shed with a fragrant smell.
She added rose geranium leaves and
lemon.   Irma asked, What do you do?
I teach English. I also help with the
farm. It'll be ready in an hour. Come to
the house. We'll drink tea.   Phim drank
two cups and ate ten small biscuits,
feeling happy with Turkey.   Irma, Yaeli,
and Aisha shared a joke. Aisha gave
them a jar and said, Bon voyage.

A truck appeared alongside. It was carrying a JTB digger with tracks. In place of the scoop, there was a hand with hydraulically-powered metal fingers, covered with black latex. The truck moved in front. The digger came to life. The hand reached over and tapped the Merc's roof. Phim was in the front next to Sal. The metal fingers prodded and then smashed the windscreen and reached inside towards Phim, grabbing him around the head. The grip tightened. It began to drag Phim out through the broken windscreen. Phim yelled, Get it off me!

Another truck appeared over the edge of the hill. The road was not very wide. It was ramshackle, carrying an upright spit used for Doner Kebab. There was tall heating element alongside, powered by an electric motor and generator. Phim, meanwhile, was suffering excruciating pressure on the skull as he tried to wriggle free. Inside that skull, he cried to God. He put Greek and Arabic together, shouting: Allah Theos! The element came alive, the truck hit a hole, the doner-spit flew, piercing the hydraulics, the hand relaxed, Sal braked, Phim collapsed, holding his head, groaning.

They were looking at the terraced houses. Yaeli said, What the super-rich Ephesians enjoyed is what we all want. Sal said, The Romans began the modern world. Phim said, I like the mosaics. The shopping mall floors had swirling designs with red, white, orange and blue. The orange was a ribbon and the other colours were bold circling lines. A white Greek cross in the centre — was that a Christian artisan? A section with hexagonal lozenges contained geometrical interlinked shapes. The complex patterns were an oriental carpet. Red and orange gave the general tone of the floor.

Joseph said, Remember Acts? Paul was here.   Phim said, Yes, it's vividly written. He'd been here for up to three years teaching. He'd been achieving miracles, but there was a reaction against him. The old temple was the lifeblood. A large mob in the theatre wanted to lynch him and companions. He spoke but they shouted him down. The city must have been split. It's as if a long history is compressed into a few lines.   Joseph said, Some of the content might be disguised. When it says synagogue what does it mean? Who followed him first?

(Acts of the Apostles 18-19.)

The huge amphitheater was almost empty. Phim was taken by the desire to sing. Yaeli and Irma, go up to the highest level. Let's see what the acoustics are like. They ran up to the top level, some 25 meters away. Phim launched into a favorite. "O sole mio, sta nfronte a te!" Irma shouted, Truly terrible. Stop! "It's now or never, come hold me tight!" Yaeli shouted, It's simply too cruel. Two off-duty Turkish police women appeared, looking amused. He stopped abruptly and started to examine a pillar. The police woman said, Çok güzel! But not permitted, sorry.

("My sun is your face." Neapolitan song 1898. "It's Now or Never." Elvis Presley 1960. Çok güzel! Very good.)

The proportions of the ancient temple were huge — approximately 130 m by 70 m, with a double row of columns marching round an inner sanctum, with vestibule, cella with altar and enormous statue, and inner sanctum behind. The site was now a marshy wilderness. A stork's nest adorned a single column. When the Christians got control, they would have used the army to pull it down. They took the stone for the Basilica. When did it happen? It must have been a fierce contest c. 330-430. The council proclaiming "Mary Mother of God" (431) signaled victory.

Phim said, Can we be sure these are the ancient statues? The Byzantines taught that she was demonic, but she could not have been. Cybele, an Asian-Anatolian Mother-Fertility goddess, blended with Greek Artemis, the beautiful huntress, the moon, the chaste one. Irma said, Look at those breasts! They are fruits, she is a tree of life. Yaeli said, Date palm, or fig or grape.   Sudan said, Life given and sustained by Mother-Earth. Why lions?   Phim said, They drew the chariot of Cybele. Fierce guardians. I feel how much they loved her. Our peoples blended; she became.

(Ephesus Archaeological Museum. Statues of Artemis of Ephesus.)

Phim found out more. Artemis was a chaste female hunter. How puzzling. Don't peep at her in the nude. Moon? Forest animals were sacrificed to her. Apollo's twin sister. He was sun, arts, healing. A pair for city and forest? She had to be pure to be worthy of killing the deer — an ancient memory from the hunter-gatherers? Blended with Cybele, a fertility goddess. Agriculture. She was called mother of the gods. Mountain and plain; hunter and farmer. Taker and giver of life? The most ferocious beast protected Asian Cybele; but Artemis hunted the beasts in the colder woods.

Pope Benedict had written a message celebrating the pilgrimage site as a place for peace for both Christians and Muslims. Sal said, Christians forget that Saint Mary is important in Islam. She has many verses in the Quran. Irma said, It's good to have this site here, close to Ephesus. Joseph said, Look at the large baptismal pool. It was a hidden Christian community in the forest. Mary mother of the church. They declared her Divine Motherhood in Ephesus (431) to bring the ancient devotion to God. Phim said, The holy work of Christ. The old devotion was very strong.

(Marian Shrine, Mary House: Meryemana Evi, Bülbüldağı, 7 km from Selçuk. Benedict XVI 1927-2022.)

Mary's house had been reconstructed and repaired through the ages. It was originally a cross-shape. They'd used stone blocks and brick tiles. Inside, there was an altar with a statue of Mary and a candle. Only eight people were allowed in. They stood there silent. Irma sang softly in Coptic. Mary, blessed dove, pray for us, amen. The candle flame moved in the gentle breeze. The crown on the statue shone in the light from the window. Phim thought, Mother Mary, all the goodness of faith.   Outside, they went to the holy spring.   Sal said, Phim?   Please, said Phim.

(House seen in vision by German nun Anne Catherine Emmerich 1774-1824.)

Phim was listening to a Turkish folksong. It was a song about Zeynep, which was the Turkish for Arabic Zainab, meaning fragrant flower. The song was yearning. It was sad and passionate. She was descended from beauty; her thoughts were beauty. Beauty was a code word for Allah. It must be suggesting Zainab, the grandaughter of Muhammad. It was too far away. She was now a bride. It was an allegory. Had he been thinking of taking a holy wife, which would mean becoming an Imam? The bağlama strummed and the voice called out in love and grief.

("Zeynep bu güzellik var mı soyunda?" Anonymous. Sung by Nazlı Öksüz (1972 -) Turkish folksinger.
For Zainab, see Samawatiwal'ard epis. 195-196.)

Joseph said, The tale of the seven sleepers was a very popular legend, mentioned in the Quran (18.9-26) and in pious Christian books, most famously in the Golden Legend. The Quran indicates debate on the number of sleepers and years asleep, and says the answer rests with God. There's a point. In this cave, they excavated hundreds of fourth and fifth century terracotta oil lamps with Christian and pagan symbols. It was a burial site during the transition time. It points to the shared belief in resurrection of the faithful with God — goodness brings you to heaven.

(See Exnihil episode 271. Yedi Uyuyanlar, Cave Tomb on Panayır Dağı, Mt Pion.)

Phim said, Is it possible that the seven churches of Revelation are the seven stars of the Pleiades, with seven angels shining? To someone with exceptional eyesight and a knowledge of geography, the star-pattern could seem to be a map. Star-knowledge was pagan but the Church would want it to be Christian. Sal said, Many of these places were pagan sanctuaries. Joseph said, The seven churches offer an allegory. They're a chain that must not be broken. They must be a string of pearls. Yaeli said, Maybe the star-pattern outlines a doorway. "Here I am. I stand at the door."

(Revelation 3.20)

Phim said, No one ever comments that the Biblical visions have much in common with pagan imagery. The blazing eyes of Christ. Bronze feet. The four Gospel creatures seem terrifyingly Egyptian. Mighty wings were found on Isis or Assyrian lions. Joseph said, It's obvious why not. For the Jews also, you could imagine God if you dare, but you mustn't draw or sculpt Him. It was dangerously misleading to the simple people, who treated such artifacts as having power. Sal said, That's the reason surely, but if you viewed a cow intellectually as a holy sign, wouldn't that be OK?

(E·

One of the best preserved Hellenistic theatres, dating to c. 300 BCE.   Phim said, Look at the principal seats, called Prohedria. Marble thrones for the priests with lion-paws carved on the arm-rests. Guardians? There's an altar. It's a temple.   The guide said, Live animals were sacrificed to Dionysios.   Sudan said, If you replaced the animal sacrifices with a decent ritual, surely this design would be the best.   Sal said, All would be assembled. We could focus on the message. There'd be a sense of unity. Yaeli said, Too democratic, isn't it? Too educational. Not enough mystery.

(Priene, Güllübahçe, Söke, opposite Miletus.)

Paul summoned the Ephesus elders. Once thriving centers of Greek civilization and pagan pilgrimage would later become Byzantine Christian hubs (Ephesus, Pergamum, Miletus). There were once philosophers in Miletus — the so-called Milesian school (c. 500 BCE). They said it was the beginning of science ... Why were they so clever? ... The elders wept because they knew they would never see Paul's face again. "Face" is often used with a holy sense of God's presence. Did they feel that the Lord Jesus was alive in Paul? Ephesus meets Miletus. Paul is a Holy Being for them. Phim wondered about it.

(Acts 20.15-17; Acts 14.12; Acts 28.6.)

The scale of the sanctuary was astonishing. Phim said, These columns are massive. I'd like to know more about how they built these places. Is that really how high it was? How did they put the architrave on top? Sal said, The whole community expended themselves - a holy task, like ancient Egypt or the English Cathedrals. This is what the Artemision would have been like. Phim said, Ephesus Artemis the twin of Didyma Apollo. Was that the point? Joseph said, Moon and Sun. There were about seven ancient Pagan sanctuaries on this holy coast, a pagan pilgrimage zone.

(Didyma Temple of Apollo c. 300 BCE very important oracle of Greek religion.)

Phim was reading the Book of Revelation, and imagined Christ walking between the lamp stands, seeing a handsome priest, aged about 33, dark brown complexion, bearded, with flowing hair. He cast myrrh on the coals and clouds of incense billowed up. Smyrna, which had become Izmir, came from Myrrh. Prosperous through trade arriving on the Silk Road. Myrrh was treasure, like the purple dye from Tyre. Caravans had brought it up from the Yemen. Izmir stood opposite Athens. Trade developing from the time of Alexander, flourishing under the Romans. Who was buying this precious spice, a gift for a king?

(Rev 1.12-13) (Heb. mōr; LXX σμύρνα, smurna: myrrh.)

Phim found a videoclip. A man in a blue shirt with bright eyes explained, Domitian the Emperor. His beloved infant son died. He deified him, and issued a medal (82-83 CE). They showed the medal. An orb (the globe?) wrapped in a cross. A naked child sat on it, arms held out, candelabra or star-like hands, four stars left, three right. Domitia the mother shown with staring eyes. Grief. Tenderness. Phim felt a pang. Her son was in the heavens among the stars. She put him there. How she'd loved him! Romans would have treasured this. What about Jews?

(With thanks to Joe Stowell's "Our Daily Bread" presentation. Silver denarius (82-83 CE) featuring deified infant son.)

Phim said, Revelation admonishes the Churches for eating food sacrificed to idols. Is that possible?   Joseph said, This is a theme in Paul's letters and Revelation. Who would eat such food? Normally, the pagan clergy would eat such food. Obviously they're not in a temple. It might be in a large household, which offers regular sacrifice to household gods: food given to the Christian slaves, who are poor? Or Christian citizens taking part in civic functions in which food is offered and then used in a feast. It would be a transition time. Christian and Pagan citizens are feasting together.

(Acts 15.20; Acts 15.29; Acts 21.25; 1 Cor. 8.1-13; Rev. 2.14; Rev. 2.20.)

The guide showed them the Pergamum Library, with how many hundred thousand scrolls. Phim remembered the facade of the Celsus Library at Ephesus, and then thought again of the Alexandrian Library. Where had he read just now how they'd made a bonfire of magic books? In the public square? So many thousand years of research into herbs, trying them out on the slaves, lessons learned, all lost. Ah Egypt! Your advanced intelligence in those temples along the Nile. The guide now took them to the Asclepium. Maybe they did have better healing techniques that we simply don't know about.

(Acts 19.19; June 17, 1242 Paris.)

Phim looked into a sacred temple floor, shaped like a square. What's he doing here, wreathing and writhing? Phim called Sudan.   The Asclepian snake, said Sudan. The Greeks thought the snakes were powerful healers filled with earth-wisdom. It was an Egyptian connection;   or   Pan-Mediterranean. Yaeli said, Perfectly obvious what it meant.   Sal said, Wisdom is good but knowledge is sometimes poisonous. Irma   said,   Ancient   upstanding guardians?   Sudan said, These ones are harmless. What a beautiful sheen they have. The early peoples loved all kinds of snakes. Look how they wriggle and speed along. How they are reborn in new-skin.

(Numbers 21.4-9; John 3.14-15; Asclepius Greek god of healing; Zamenis longissimus, the Asclepian snake.)

They were talking about Revelation. Joseph said, It was a hard time. The newly established Church gave strong guidance. We don't talk about the cost. Irma said, It's good to learn about it. Grief for suffering is good. It's true that the loving gift of God is better. Sudan said, Too much destruction. Too much waste. The more I learn the angrier I get. Phim said, I do regret the loss of beauty. It is God's key. Sal said, We need the gentle teacher of science, filled with green strength. Yaeli said, The true rabbi, green to the core.

(Church established 300-600; paganism abolished.)

Phim said, The honor, the glory, the courage and the waste of war — how patiently Homer took his time to make his point. Burn the most beautiful city and put them all to the sword? Begin with anger. Agamemnon scorns a priest who pleads for his daughter. The priest prays, "O hear me, Apollo, master of the silver bow, if ever to your liking in any grove I roofed a shrine or burnt fat on your altar!" Apollo walked with storm in his heart. The bowstring thrummed. The arrows of the god rained down on the Achaeans.

(Adapted from Homer, *Iliad* 1.1-50. Robert Fitzgerald trans. OUP, 1984. Achaeans: Greeks.)

O childish rage, your funeral pyres burn forever, Ilium herself will be a burning pyre. "As Achilles slid the blade from the sheath, Athena came to him from the sky. The white-armed goddess, Hera, sent her, she loved them both. Athena stepped up behind him and gripped his golden hair. He made a half-turn. He knew instantly it was her. Terribly her blue-grey eyes blazed at him. Speaking softly he said, O daughter of the god of heaven who bears the storm-cloud, why are you here? She replied, To check this killing rage I came."

(Adapted from Homer, *Iliad* 1.190-210. Robert Fitzgerald trans. OUP, 1984.)

Sal said, Phim, do you remember this glorious passage? "All night long the watchfires blazed among them, as stars in the night sky when the air falls to a windless calm, as when from heaven all the stars shine clear, and the shepherd's heart exults — so many fires burned between the ships and the Xanthus' whirling rapids, and beside each fire sat fifty fighting men, waiting for Dawn to mount her glowing throne."   There's irony here, said Yaeli, their courage may be splendid but they're all doomed. Incomparable Ilium will be lost. Beauty and grace ravaged by ignorant war.

(Adapted from Homer, *Iliad* 8.640 ff. Robert Fagles trans. Penguin,1990.)

As they drove along, Phim turned from Homer to Shakespeare. A line he once knew. "In the heart or in the head?" He pondered a moment, remembering his old teacher expounding "imagination." A good lesson. He'd forgotten that. Later, he met the word again in the Romantics course. Coleridge said something about it. To strike analogies and make resemblance; she will spring from one to the other like an electric spark and be seen brightest in her leaping. The living power and prime agent of human perception. Then a singing line came to mind, the true is most feigning.

Before his very eyes the screen, with its showing of the ancient walls and foundations, the room in which the elders sat, the marble flooring, the original a blueprint for the future, as he watched, a finger whittled away the content, both the beginning and the continuation, telling Phim very clearly (here was the paradox) that God, the true love of God, existed in the love between you and me, Christian and Muslim and Jew. The opponent was alive. The screen was blank. The gentle voice of explanation gone. Phim searched for it but could not find it.

Phim struggled with himself, rent in two, thinking of how they had gotten through before. Focus once again. Why do I have to forget? Why can't I hold it? Focus it, hard, stronger, he called within himself to God, crying: Lord God restore this me, lead me to you; he shouted Allah, the beautiful name, Allah, O Theos, and a shattering boom of thunder within him broke through, the screen rebuilt itself, there was the place they sat, in that hard time, composing a word to achieve heaven. I believe in one God, the maker of heaven and earth.

The authority issued a statement as the Merc approached Nicaea (Iznik). A terrorist group has flooded the ancient Basilica with radioactive fluid. You cannot visit it at this time. We apologize to our visitors for this. The terrorists wish to inflame Christian feeling against Islam (and vice versa). They will perpetuate hostility. They refuse reconciliation. The authority affirms friendship once again. We will defend and restore Nicaea. Please visit later. We will build bridges between Islam and Christianity. We will oppose these acts of terror which promote hate. We know that both Islam and the Church are founded with love.

(Nicaea Council 325 key moment in the Christian story.)

The pillars of the Bosphorus Bridge, and beyond them the blue sky with white clouds. We're returning to Europe, said Phim, thinking that in fact they'd never left, how empty such categories were. The Merc hastened onwards. The sun flooded in from the left. The skyscrapers could be seen in the distance.   Can we see the Hagia Sophia?   The Bosphorus flowed like a river beneath. Wash away the dreams of conquest. Will you be my slave, or shall I be thine? The pillars lifted the bridge and God shows through, thought Phim, they spell the name.

(15 July Martyrs Bridge.)

Boom! The sound wave rocked Phim where he stood. At the same time he heard the crash of shop windows. They'd just put the Merc in the hotel car park and were taking their first stroll in Istanbul. Terror, said Ange, a faint reflection in the light. Phim was gripped by grief. Sal said, Keep together. That was a bomb. Back to the hotel. A bomb had been set off in Istiklal street. How many hurt? Chaos. Who'd done it? Sirens were now wailing, and loudhailers were telling people to keep indoors. Anxiety ran icy fingers through the guts.

(Staying in Arora hotel not far from Istiklal.)

They spent the next two days cooped up in the hotel under a curfew as they tried to sort out the terror. Rumors of wars and the beginnings of wars. There was talk about a new virus which could wipe out the human race. Should masks be issued for everyone? The authorities released the security camera footage of the bomber. A young woman in black, hooded, face hidden, hurrying through the streets leaving a shopping bag, and hurrying away. A symbol on her back. A locust head. Underneath it "Shaten." They said about ten people had been killed.

Phim leaned closer to the screen to see better what was going on, and was able to hear the thoughts of the five faith leaders who stood, linked arm in arm. To his amazement, each one was praying in their own language, and even more strange, the Imam was praying in Hebrew, the Patriarch from the Quran, the Rabbi from the Gospel. Before joining the parade, each leader had changed clothes with his brother, so that the Imam was really the Rabbi, the Patriarch the Imam, and the Rabbi the Christian. With one voice, We renounce this act of terror.

(Istanbul Faith Leaders in solidarity parade against terror.)

Phim woke with a start. Opened the hotel door, and sprinted along the corridor. He'd been dreaming of climbing a minaret, a tall pencil pointing at the stars, he shinnied up it, almost reaching the top, he could almost shake their hands. It was hard, all the city below was watching him, he heard their voices, a terrible hubbub. Then the sky filled with fireworks, Blam Blam, like a million stars and he'd awoken, and ran, for my life he thought, looking behind him, why am I running? Where am I? The joyful din pursued him, Sal where are you?

Is this heaven, asked Phim, gazing on the unbroken window display of sweetmeats. There were trays of baklava of all kinds, soaked in honey and baked golden brown. There were trays of lokum, cubes of pink and green and yellow. There were also pyramids of cannelloni with various fillings and coatings. Phim said, That one looks rather weary. He pointed to a fat tube covered in cracked peanuts which lay limply. It was filled with crema which plumped outwards. Is that originally Turkish, asked Yaeli. Sudan said, It's probably Italian. An over-adventurous combination, said Sal.

(Osmanlizadeler 1879 sweetmeats & pastries Istiklal.)

Walking on ahead of them was a man carrying a basket of cloths and brushes. He dropped a brush on the pavement and walked on, appearing not to have noticed. A black shoe brush with black bristles. Phim bent down to pick it up to return it to him. Alarm bells rang. They'll use your love to destroy you. He thrust it away and picked it up, Must try to be decent, and suddenly saw a large square black rock. A bright sunny day. Round and round we go joyfully thankfully. The shoeshiner smiled and moved on quickly.

They were looking at paintings by
Osman Hamdi. "The Two Musician
Girls" (1880). Sal said, He loved the
robes. Look at how beautiful they are!
This one's famous. "The Tortoise
Trainer" (1906). Haha, said Sudan, you
can't train tortoises. Phim said, Maybe
you could with infinite patience.
Joseph said, It's a joke. He's got the reed
pipe on this back. He must be a Sufi
teacher. These are the disciples. Yaeli
said, Two set off right, three wait on left.
His turban in the height. A verse above
his head. Sal said, God is the light! It's
a holy niche.

(Osman Hamdi 1842-1910. "The healing of hearts is meeting with the beloved.")

The chef shaved off chicken from the doner kebab with an iron-shaped plane. Chicken in a pitta bread roll.   Phim said, It needs ketchup.   A bit further down the street, they went into a Simit shop. Sal ordered borek with minced beef.   Sal said, I could eat five. They passed Lookanta, which offered various hot dishes.   Joseph said, I'd like some stuffed vine leaves. I'll take four.   At Hafiz Mustafa, Yaeli said, I'll try the trileçe (fluffy sponge with three kinds of milk syrup).   Me too, chorused the others. They sat and drank Turkish tea and watched the crowds.

(Chicken durum, stuffed borek, stuffed vine leaves, trileçe.)

Phim said, Stained glass with brilliant colors, reminiscent of Victorian windows. They'd removed the window-covers. Sun blazed through. Sal said, Obviously a grand restoration has been going on in Istanbul. Each mosque has its own color-scheme. Phim said, The dome is amazing. It's a sunflower with a dark blue disc with shining verses swirling around the centre-point. Sudan said, Like stars moving. Irma said, Twelve rays from the sun reach toward the windows. It's a clock. Yaeli said, Look, there's a cross-shape within a double-square, and a flower-shape, surely angels. Joseph said, Two different kinds of angel.

(Mimar Sinan designed Mosque 1555 for Sinan Pasha, an admiral. Beshiktash.)

They were comparing two nineteenth century mosques, the Ortaköy (1856) and Dolmabahçe (1855). The Ortaköy looks like an ornate European palace, said Phim.   The interior was notably so. Elegance, taste, large beige panels, golden calligraphy, it harked back one hundred years. The Ortaköy mihrab had tassle-like carving in the muqarnas. The Dolmabahçe had gold ornamentation. Sal said, I don't like too much glittering gold in the mihrab. Sometimes they go too far. It distracts. It should be a pure niche for God, our precious cool prayer-window.   Phim said, When you stand back, the gold detail glimmers in the natural light.

(Both Mosques designed by the Balyans, father and son.)

Sal said, You can point at the huge expense and ask questions about the health of the rural population (1853). Phim said, It's impressive. If I were the grandson of Turkish peasants, I'd be glad to see how beautiful it is and know that it belongs to me.   Irma said, Modern Turkey is a wonderful country. Yaeli said, It was a hard birth. A long birth.   Joseph said, Increasing liberalism is opening up the doors for both Christianity and Islam. Look at this beautiful chandelier. A symbol.   Sudan said, Green issues press strongly. Will someone put on the green light!

(Dolmabahçe Imperial Hall chandelier.)

They'd switched it on. Phim gasped at it. Sal said, Look how it recalls the muqarnas in the mosque. Irma said, Like icicles or water dripping or suspended. Sudan said, A galaxy of white-gold stars. Joseph said, An array of candles standing above the water. Yaeli said, It's a vision of how things ought to be, were the world as it ought to be. The royals had that vision but it was wrongly offered; but the vision remains true. It was there from the beginning. I see them standing there in golden array, they are above the water.

(Said to be the world's largest Bohemian crystal chandelier.)

They were looking closely at the iron railings by the sea, which had been covered in thick paint. Sudan said, It must be weather-resistant modern paint. Sal said, Look how close to the sea the palace is placed, and the Ortakoy Mosque the same. Irma said, It looks like Venice, doesn't it? Phim said, What happens if there's a storm? Sudan said, The wind is most often from the north, otherwise from the east. Summer is calm with breezes. February is windy. Storms are rare, but if there are, waves are channeled down the narrow strait, not striking the land.

It was a national holiday. Phim said, There are many Turkish holidays which celebrate the Republic. Sal said, Turkey was like a newborn nation (1923). Sudan said, It's time we had globally conscious holidays. How about International Green Day? Irma said, Are there any such holidays? Sudan said, There's "World Environment Day" (June 5). No one's made it a national holiday. It's already 50 years old. Yaeli said, Their website says "Beat Plastic Pollution." Joseph said, That's a faith issue, surely. The world we share. Protect it. Phim said, Planet Earth is a Holy House. Be good. Clean it up.

(April 22 is Earth Day. Japan has "Green Day" May 4 and other "green" holidays.)

As they strolled in the suburbs, they passed a pre-school. Irma looked through the window. There was a class of 5 year olds singing in English and Turkish. A young woman was wearing a long blue hat with a golden bell. "Make way for Noddy," they sang, and then sang in Turkish. On the screen they showed Toyland. What a lovely song, said Yaeli. Phim said, It's Enid Blyton, written originally in the 1950s, still very popular. He stood and watched with the children. Old friends were speaking Turkish. There was Big Ears! PC Plod. Tessa the Bear.

We started in Istanbul in 1949. Baklava was not as well known then among ordinary people, being once a special treat from Topkapi for the Janissaries. It probably came from Ancient Greece, with cheese and honey on a pastry base, then refined by the Ottomans. The Ottomans loved good cooks. Look. The chef held up the thin diaphanous pastry. The bright red Turkish flag showed through. Fragrant vivid green pistachio. Layered on pastry. Melted butter. Abundant syrup. Little golden square domes. Pistachio still green within. Please have one, said the chef.

(Inspired by Nadir Güllü. Karaköy Güllüoğlu. Baklava specialists.)

Phim said, The first domed Christian Church that was built after the conquest (1453). The bell towers were also permitted. It was the Tanizmat period - liberalization.   Sal said, I feel God's hand in liberalization.   Yaeli said, Me too.   Joseph said, The first Christian dome in 400 years.   Phim said, Left and right we assert ownership. The dome is ours. Mother is ours. Father is ours. The holy name is ours. The song is ours, not yours.   Irma said, The dome decoration is Christian and Islamic. How wonderful! Christ is a gentle Greek-Turk liberal blessing the world. Cherubim all around.

(Holy Trinity Greek Orth. Church, Taksim 1880. Another beautiful Holy Trinity in Kadikoy 1905, architect Velissarios Makropoulos.)

It was bright weather. They stood looking at the Galata Bridge in Karakoy. That must be the Beyazit tower in Istanbul campus. Looks like a candle, said Yaeli. Above the city, the Rustem Pasha Mosque glowed pale yellow in the sun. Irma said, You know, it looks a bit like a huge seated figure, the round dome could be the head. Galata bridge was packed with fishing rods, the lines glittered in the still air. Lines from the sky, said Sal. Huge ferries moved slowly to rest. Phim gazed peacefully on the Bosphorus, mesmerized by the waters reflecting the light.

Yaeli read from the guidebook, Ayyub El Ansari, called Eyüp Sultan by the Turks, was the Prophet Muhammad's standard-bearer and companion. He died outside the walls in the first siege of Constantinople (c. 670). Centuries later, when Mehmed had taken the city (1453) his ancient tomb was rediscovered. They built a mosque (1458). This is where the new Sultan received his sword of sovereignty. They stood by the tomb, surrounded by pilgrims. There were two Senegalese with shining heads. The tiles were highly ornate and colorful, with calligraphy. Phim said, This expensive work shows the Ottoman's pious intention.

(Rebuilt 1800.)

Yaeli read from the guidebook. Sinan masterpieces (c. 1548 & c. 1566). Mosque complexes with school, bath, fountain, hospital, bazaar — the Ottoman charitable gift. In this we outshine Rome. Strong-willed Princess Mihrimah (1522-78) was the daughter of Suleyman and Roxelana. Sinan is said to have been in love with her. She married Rustem Pasha, the grand vizier. Sinan built her two mosques, on either side of the Bosphorus. In Persian, "mihr" means "sun," "mah" means "moon." On her birthday, March 21 the sun rises by her Üsküdar mosque and sets by the one in Edirnekapı, and the moon follows.

(Mihrimah Mosque, Edirnekapı. Former slave Roxelana rose to become favorite wife. There are two Mihrimah Mosques.)

Four-side cube carrying a dome. Large arched tympana on each wall with plentiful windows. The wall is an aqueduct carrying the glass windows. Is this the most light-filled of Sinan's mosques? How much light-energy gets through? It must be hot in the summer. Good in the winter. They don't need oil-lamps in the daytime. A wall of light above the mihrab. The stained glass windows have green leaf and red blossoms. Jeweled windows with green and blue panels. They say it has a feminine atmosphere. Peaceful, thought Phim, in his heart, as he said, Thank you God.

(Mihrimah Mosque, Edirnekapı.)

Princess Mihrimah and Roxelana were both charitable. Phim asked the Imam, What does the Quran say about charity? Helping the poor or afflicted is charity, said the Imam. Islam is adamant on this. You must give to help others. It is also charity to build a Mosque, as it is for a Christian to build a church. "Those who spend their wealth in Allah's cause are like grains of wheat which produce seven ears, each bearing a hundred grains." Recognize the metaphor? The Gospel is wary of the dangers of wealth; the Quran says, use your wealth for God.

(Quran 2:261. See Mt 13.23; Mk 10.23–25.)

Phim said, Please help us to understand the concept of God. The Imam said, God is not something you can grasp with your five senses. You can feel or know or read. This helps you. We have glimmering hints. We have holy words. Islam and the Churches both share the same God. Both share a similar structure. A learned priesthood and people. Both progressed from a primitive idea to a more advanced concept. Both were children, now adult. Both were fighters, now peaceful. No image, no word, no created wonder, no mind can truly speak the reality of God (Allah).

(Inspired by Dr Shabir Ally "Let the Quran Speak.")

The Imam said, I have a friend here, who became Muslim in France a couple of years ago. She's a model who's been on reality TV. A tall willowy North African beauty bowed to Phim and said, Delighted to meet you, with a French accent. Islam is growing in France. At the same time Islam is becoming more French. Many of my friends are Catholic. Imams and Priests are working together increasingly to combat the loss of faith. We both proclaim God. We can love Mary. We can love God. My brother became an Imam; my sister a Christian.

The Imam said, I've attended interfaith conferences in Geneva and Rome. How can we promote dialogue between faiths, for the purpose of peace and love? In Turkey especially (and elsewhere) Islam does not follow a militaristic conquistadorial ideology. It was the old world. Christians ask me, why was Islam given by God? I reply, Put aside all thought of conflict, recrimination, set ideas. Listen as I sing His name and rejoice in the light through the Mihrimah windows. My brother, my sister, it is the same God. Yes, said Phim, I feel this is true. The height is God.

The Imam said, I studied English Literature for a year in England. Shakespeare. Our teacher showed us how Henry V could be viewed. That word about religion from Marlowe or Ralegh. Self-belief is important. All for this glorious cause. Machiavelli? Ottomans and infidels and vice-versa. The ancient Roman legionary, driven by self-belief and fear, hardened, stocky, standing firm as the fortieth desperate Celt runs against him and falls. *Magnificent Century* was a mirror, have you seen it? Mature art, complex values, the ability to love both sides: "I believe I love you" is what God says to me.

(The "Baine's Note," perhaps a forgery, 1593. Nicolo Machiavelli 1469-1527. Cp Wolf Hall 2015. Magnificent Century 2011-2014. TV drama Turkey.)

Sal said, What a puzzling mosaic. They were looking at the icon of the donor Theodore Mitochites (1270-1332), the Emperor's treasurer, presenting Christ with the monastery. It echoed the icon in Hagia Sophia of Justinian offering the cathedral.   Yaeli said, Is that a turban? The notes explained that costume in 1320 had been influenced by the east.   Phim said, It's an allegory. The turban represents the cosmos, his face is the sun, those are beams of light. The heavens acknowledge the supremacy of Christ.   Irma said, How about, my church and my mind I give to you?

(Chora Monastery. Inscription reads: "Jesus Christ, the dwelling-place (chora) of the living.")

They were looking at a mosaic of Christ in the nave. The face had been damaged. His light brown hair and rosy cheek could be seen. The long dark blue robes suggested water. He held open a large Bible. Matthew 11:28. "Come to me, all you who are weary and burdened, and I will give you rest." It was in Greek. Look, said Phim, it finishes with "kago a." Joseph said, "I" and the next word would be "will give you rest (anapavso)." Haha, said Phim, I am "A" alpha. I will give you myself, God. Allah, said Sal.

(Chora Monastery. κἀγώ   kagó: "I" emphatic.)

On the other side stood a mosaic icon, companion to that of Christ. Much had been lost.   Joseph said, It says "Mother the Chora." Mary held her infant and looked on him with sorrowful emotion. He looked up at her with a mature solemn face. His right hand blessing, the fingers spelt his name in Greek, two fingers touched to show his nature, God and man. He was wrapped in gold. Mary wore dark blue.   Irma said, Mother and son. Their eyes form a unity of love.

(Chora Monastery. χώρα chora: space or room; proper place or post; land, country.)

They were admiring the icon of Saint Paul in the Narthex.   Phim said, Surely they must have restored it considerably. Joseph said, It looks like it. The detail is too fine.   Sal said, It's a splendid icon. A study in gold and brown. Paul is quite brown.   Irma said, The eye is wonderfully expressive and kind.   Yaeli said, The beard is positively alive and curly.   Sudan said, They've done the brow very well. Look at the circular lines. Big thinking Paul.   Joseph said, He's looking at someone. Is it Tim? Lydia? Peter maybe.

(Chora Monastery.)

Irma said, Look, it's Saint Anna praying. Joseph said, These icons showing the life of the Virgin Mary are sourced from the Evangelion of Saint James, which is found in the Quran. Saint Anna in red robes stands in front of her house in Jerusalem. She sees a mother bird bringing food for her young. There's Gabriel above the tree, bringing her the good news that her prayer has been answered. Mary will be born! There's Anna and Joachim embracing before Jerusalem. The birth scene is marvellous. How many midwives! There's a message in the word midwife.

(Chora Monastery. μαῖα maia: good mother; nurse; foster-mother; midwife.)

Joseph said, This is a well-known fresco-icon. It's obviously been restored. What a triumphant work of holy art. It represents the Paschal hymn: "Christ tramples down death, bestowing life on those in the tombs." Look at the broken locks and bars. He pulls Adam and Eve out of the tomb. If you squint at it from afar you might see a hidden image. Dressed in white, within the holy aura blue and white, bright with golden stars, his legs striding over life and death, Christ strikes a dramatic figure: the Father in action, fulfilling the glorious verses of Isaiah.

(Chora Monastery. Isaiah 42.7; 61.1.)

Joseph said, The walls were breached twice, first by the Fourth Crusade (1204), second by Mehmed the Conqueror (1453). Accounts of what happens during a long siege and after the collapse supply the truest portrait of Hell. The squeamish should not read them. A siege was not, however, an infrequent happening. They would occur every few decades. Megiddo (c. 1450 BCE); Carthage (c. 150 BCE); Jerusalem (how many times); Granada (1491); Tenochtitlán (1521).   Phim said, The conquest mentality; prizes won by force; glory and honour before my friends. The same brutal lesson, again and again. Ignoble world.

(Visiting the Adrianople Gate where the walls were breached.)

Three men appeared in the Gate, wearing white Tshirts with the word "Fillhell" in black. One with Turkish mustaches; another with a Grecian nose. Phim shouted, Sal! Trouble! They had large drugged eyes, faces contorted by rage. A power possessed them with the will to destroy, driving them on. Kill! Kill! Kill! They grabbed Phim and threw him into their white van and drove off. Get in, shouted Sal, and set off in the Merc in pursuit. They were heading out of Istanbul towards the Bosphorus Martyr's bridge. They raced onto the highway, the Merc keeping pace.

(The Gate of Charisius or the Adrianople Gate.)

The van skidded to a halt at the mid-point of the bridge. The three men got out, man-handling Phim. One cuffed him. He fell, stunned. The Merc arrived. They leapt out. Sal furious. Yaeli, Sudan, Joseph. Irma hung back, praying. Mustaches was quick and strong, parrying Sal, landing a punch, dodging Yaeli's flying kick. Sudan was matched with the Greek nose. Joseph was having problems with the other, thin hair in a tail. Sal in trouble; Yaeli kicked Mustaches hard; he was out cold. Quick to help Joseph. Sal grabbing hair-tail. They grappled for a moment. Phim stood up.

The big fellow with the hair-tail broke free from Sal. He lifted Phim and sprinted to the side and threw him over. No time to think. By some blessed chance Phim plummeted down feet first, pointing his toes like a ballet dancer, raising his arms to heaven. In the split second given him, his mind raced, he took a quick breath and shouted within, God let me live! and whooosh, his toes struck the surface, a shock wave went through, he plunged deep into the cold brisk water, and pulled to the light, alive!

The battle continued. Irma ran to the side and looked over. Phim! She yelled. Far below, bobbing like a cork, rapidly moving south in the current, Phim waved up at her. Swim to the shore! Watch out for ships! Phim took off his shoes, and started to struggle to the western shore. If I'm lucky, it'll carry me to Istanbul. Sal in a mad fury threw his assailant to the ground. Sudan knocked Greek-nose out cold. Mustaches slept peacefully. Into the Merc, quick, along the coast. ... There he is, look, dripping, bedraggled, weary. Dolmabahçe Palace 3 km from the bridge.

The guide said, There was an ancient holy spring called Hagiasma. Empress Augusta Pulcheria had a church built upon it (c. 450 CE). By 474, Emperor Leo I added a marble statue of Mary, from whose hands flowed the holy spring water, as well as a sacred pool. He added the Hagia Soros chapel to house the Virgin Mary relics, which included the holy robe found by citizens on a Jerusalem pilgrimage, and a gold and silver icon of Mary. This icon, Blachernitissa, paraded along the battlements during the Avar siege (626), is credited with saving the city.

(St. Mary of Blachernae, Ayvansaray.)

They stood in front of the holy spring. There was a large marble box with the message "Wash the sins not the eyes only." Five silver taps for the spring water. There was a tray of small plastic bottles you could take away. To the left an opening looked down to a rocky channel, said to connect with Balikli, the other spring. On the left of the iconostasis a modern Blachernitissa held up her hands. Thinking upon the history they'd learned, Phim said, Let's drink the healing water and pray peace for Istanbul.

The guide said, The original icon and relics were lost in the fire of 1434. Many copies were made. The original was the Orans type, with hands upraised. We have a Byzantine cameo lent to us by the Kremlin (Constantinople 11th c.). Mary with hands upraised in prayer, carved in chalcedony, set in pure gold, with jewels and pearls around. Eight jewels, an octagon. Large red jewel with hinge. It was displayed in procession for its powerful protection. A gift for a king. Irma said, Mother and infant in the church. Joseph said, The red jewel must be Holy Spirit.

297   Rejoice!

All around the chamber voices echoed in acclamation, calling upon the Blessed Virgin to rejoice. She was to rejoice because her supreme holiness merited the task of bearing and raising Jesus to become the savior of all humanity. Phim thought, What need to call her to rejoice? We are calling ourselves to rejoice in her. Just as she declares that God remembered his mercy in helping his servant Israel — what need for God to remember, who knows all? We must remember the merciful love of God. Rejoice! Rejoice! the voices cried, describing Mary with phrases of mystical joy.

(See "The Akathist to the Holy Theotokos." Also Lk 1.54)

It was called the "Bloody Church" in Turkish, referring to the fierce resistance of the Greeks in the last hours of the struggle (1453). It had been allowed to remain a church. Founded by Maria Palaiologina, widow of Abaqa, the Mongol Khan, who'd favored Christians. Phim had just read Runciman and trembled with grief. Are we defined by the history we tell ourselves? What we endured — if we repeat to ourselves our precious story - will we ever be free? He thought of communities who had to escape untouchable status. The slave trade. God help us break these chains, thought Phim.

(Kanlı Kilise. Steven Runciman, *The Fall of Constantinople 1453*. CUP, 1965.)

Phim said, Looks like a castle. It was holiday season. No students. They were allowed to visit. Phew, said Phim, steep staircases. You'd get fit just studying here. It looked like a Victorian British public school. Built in redbrick brought from Marseille with ornate neo-gothic and classical elements. An elegant dome. A grand statement of confidence for the Greek community. The plan looked like a flying cherubim. It was now co-educational. Phim said, How good it would be to link up in exchange with leading UK or Japanese schools. How interesting it might be to study in Istanbul.

(Greek Orthodox College, Phanar 1883)

Phim said, Time for a bit of study of Turkish Delight. Irma said, I cannot think it good to have too much. Yaeli said, It's called lokum. Sal said, I'm with Phim. Sudan said, Me too. The shop owner kindly explained. It was a refined Ottoman luxury. Starch gel, traditionally flavored with rose water. Dusted with white sugar. Beautiful, isn't it. Here you can see the varieties. Phim said, Are those free samples? Allow your humble servant to compare six or seven. Hmm rose water's good, pistachio's fine, maybe the mint, ooo the chocolate, wow the orange, yesyesyes the fig!

(Turkish Delight shop in Balat)

Yaeli said, How good it feels here. This was originally a Romaniotes Jewish Synagogue (from Ohrid). They assimiliated with the Sephardim who arrived in Istanbul from Spain after 1492. This is the famous boat-shaped tevah, (also called a bimah — lectern). More than 550 years of the Jewish faith! Phim said, Yaeli, please sing some Hebrew. She stood in the tevah and sang: "Way yōtsi'eni lammerkhāv; yə khal lətseni, ki khāfets bi." "He brought me out into a broad place; he delivered me, because he delighted in me." Phim looked up to the ark, the golden letters dancing.

(Psalm 18.19)

Phim said, A church made entirely of cast iron. They looked at some old postcards. Sal said, You can see rust leaking through. You'd have no fear about earthquakes but you'd have to watch for rust. I wonder how long it would be safe? It had been refurbished. The domes were plated with gold. It looked splendid.   Sudan said, Iron is mighty. For good, for bad, it's been the most important material of the last three millennia.   Joseph said, Look at those paintings in the iconostasis. The nativity. The little face of Jesus shining in a pool of white.

(St Stephen of the Bulgars, Balat 1898)

Iconostasis in gilt bronze, with modern icons of Mary and Jesus. Heavenly palace gates glittering in the candle light. Above the royal doors there was a sunburst in gilded bronze, with a golden disc from which a dove flew outwards. There were two angels beneath with bowed heads and enormous wings. Four cherubs guarded the arch either side. On the right, bright-haired Gabriel stood in white, with tall swan wings, his hand on heart, holding a lily wand. He's looking straight at me, said Phim. Yaeli said, Me too. Irma said, He's saying I am you and you are me.

(Lk 1:28 The angel went to her and said, "Rejoice, you who are highly favored! The Lord is with you.")

They were visiting the Parekklesion (funerary chapel c. 1310), now a museum, formerly part of the Fethiye Mosque, which was converted from the Pammakaristos Church. They had restored the Parekklesion. Tall domed Greek cross, Pantocrator with twelve prophets. Late Byzantium. Palaeologan revival.   Joseph said, The rawness of the brick walls and the restored mosaics make a strong contrast. Look how many saints there are. Arches and dome define the space with mathematical joy.   Irma said, Saint Antonios is holding a scroll looking thoughtful. He's the only one hooded. The border is a flourishing garden. It's been nicely restored.

(Church of Theotokos Pammakaristos reconstructed as a Mosque 1591)

As they walked through the gates Phim recognized the robed figure surrounded by people. It was Patriarch Bartholomew, whom he had watched a few times on the mobile. He looked towards them and smiled. A wise gentle face. He was the survivor of the Millennials, together with Elizabeth II, seeing the Third Millennium on its way, a counterpart to John Paul II (Pope 1978-2005). The robes stood about him like a shell of golden light. He was pale. His beard was snowy-white. Phim thought, I'd like to chat with him. Bartholomew beckoned to them, Welcome, he said.

(Bartholomew I [1940-] 270th Archbishop of Constantinople & Ecumenical Patriarch [1991-]). Pope Benedict XVI [1927-2022] also a Millennial [Pope 2005-2013]. Elizabeth II [1926-2022] reigned [1952-2022])

I'll show you St George's, said
Bartholomew. Still sailing at the gateway
of seas. It was a homely vessel, dressed
with beautiful pictures, a golden curtain
for the icons, silver icons on the stands.
Remember with me the beginning,
Phim, his eyes watered and showed pain.
Such warm gentle eyes — where have I
seen them before? He showed the
ancient throne.   A secret Phim, deep
within, the good ones love us. Storms
cease, the seas calm, a worse trial comes.
Freedom, prosperity, then ... he looked
at Sudan. You've got a job to do.
Where's Ange, he asked. What, thought
Phim.

(St George's Cathedral, Phanar)

Bartholomew said, Icons were once found in trees, or recovered by miracle from the sea. I walked alone once in a Greek forest not far from Olympus. I felt the presence of God. Orthodoxy is a high stairway, Phim. Lower rungs are basic; higher rungs are bright. Where the light breaks from the ocean, with science and old puzzling ways, and early fears and loves, we must embrace in the light. Seek it, Phim. Look what I hold in my hand. It was a jeweled picture on his breast. He opened his fingers. How beautiful, exclaimed Irma.

Incredible, said Phim.   Sal said, I sense a message in the arches and spaces. The name of God?   Joseph said, Probably. No, said Irma, laughing, can't you see? Five Turkish wrestlers arm in arm carrying a bridge of heaven!   Hahaha, said Sudan.   Phim read the guidebook, Sinan restored the first aqueduct he'd built.   Yaeli said, Suleyman praised him for filling the public fountains.   Phim said, I love this water bridge.   Sal said, Sinan innovated by widening the supporting piers to give it greater stability. They're pyramidal. It's still standing.   It's also a cathedral, said Irma, looking at an old print.

(Mağlova Aqueduct 1563 partly submerged by the Alibey reservoir 1983)

Irma said, Surely there's a message in
the silhouette of the Mosque, crowning
the city.   Phim said, It's a mountain or
hill, the minarets pointing at the stars.
Sudan said, It's the place of thought. It's
abundant mercy.   Sal said, "In the last
days the mountain of the Lord's temple
will be established." From the beginning
we find the prophetic spirit of Isaiah in
the Quran. Holy temple with a mighty
dome! A birthplace of faith! Wisdom
become peace. Hagia Sophia's holy
shape was Sinan's constant inspiration.
Phim said, It's an Isaiah house. Let's
walk in the light of God.

(Mosque of Selim II at Edirne, 1569-75. Isaiah 2.1-22)

The guide said, Eight piers support the 31 m dome, forming an octagon. They are extended upwards outside and capped with small domes. This gives the effect of surrounding the main dome with eight turrets. It looks like a crown. This decorative detail is Sinan's innovation. It dresses up the Hagia Sophia prototype. Note. From the mother dome the smaller domes cascade outwards. A strong allegory. Inside we have the brilliant polychrome Iznik tiles, the epitome of Ottoman decoration, combining fantastic Chinese clouds and saz leaves (long serrated leaf), creating a unique opulent style, suggesting also Persia.

(Mosque of Selim II at Edirne, 1569-75. Sinan considered this Mosque his masterpiece.)

On the ferry to the Prince's Islands,
Phim remembered Ange. They admired
the mosque with beautiful tiled mihrab.
They stopped in Saint John Church. It
was an ancient foundation (879). Christ
icon in silver. They stood and prayed.
They climbed through paths with
Mediterranean pines, and gazed at the
splendid view. There was a pleasant
breeze. They'd bought a picnic in the
port. Poğaça with cheese and tomatoes.
They sat on the beach, and listened to
the waves rustling on the stones. The
ancient sea of Marmara. Joseph said,
Been thinking of Ange. Irma said, I
miss him.

(Peynirli poğaça: buns with cheese filling)

Phim put his hand on the massive pillar, looking up to the domes, gazing on the detailed decoration that filled every inch. The pillars were colossal. Mighty elephant for Allah carry the dome-sky forever. They'd fitted a tap into the pillar. Phim looked about, and washed his fingers. The attendant hurried over. Not permitted.   Sorry, said Phim. The attendant said, It's a unique fountain. Water from the pillar. Holy spring from God. Are you Muslim? Phim said, I want to love and learn about Islam. There is so much good. The attendant said, Please drink the water. Cold and sweet!

(Blue Mosque 1616)

313   Blue Mosque Tiles

The walls and arches were covered in
tiles. French visitors had called it the
Blue Mosque because of the dominant
tone. The patterns were geometrical but
hinted at other things. Within an
intricate blue border red lozenges were
roses. In the dome there was a
cross-shape within swirling lines which
was a star or an angel. There was a wall
of exquisitely detailed tiles. Within
window shapes the flowers rioted in
fantastic joy, reminding Phim of the
otherworldly decoration of the
Damascus Mosque, dating back to early
Islam. It said, I will tell of the creative
wonders of God.

(Blue Mosque 1616)

Phim said to the Imam, Teach us about colors. The Imam said, Blue is respected. Turquoise-blue is specially venerated for spiritual qualities. Red is a life-force. It reflects fire and passion in positive ways. The red rose for God. White is holy and beautiful. It is praised for garments. There's a hadith attributed to Muhammad which reads, "Clothe yourselves in white. Verily, it is cleaner and purer." Green is above all the holy color. Muhammad wore a green robe. Many Muslims refrain from wearing it out of piety. Sudan said, How wonderful that Islam should teach that green is holy!

(Samurah ibn Jundab reported the Hadith. Source: Sunan al-Tirmidhī 2810)

The Imam continued. Let me teach three important words. Resurrection. Judgement. Recompense. Truth to hold and higher truth. The Hereafter is no "pie-in-the-sky," or figment of imagination. It is desirable, it is necessary, it is possible, it is real. The reality of the Hereafter compels our awareness of our long-term future. The need to work for it. Here, on earth. Your only opportunity is here and now, in this life, given once. Do good now, sow the seeds of heaven. Do you believe in God? Do you know what God means? Are you a non-believer, serving your selfish greedy will?

(Quoting from & inspired by Abdul Wahid Hamid, *Islam the Natural Way*. London: Mels, 1989.)

The Imam said, Phim, have a look at this. Pope Benedict stood with head bowed in prayer, side by side with Mustafa Çağrıcı, the Istanbul Mufti, and Emrullah Hatipoğlu, the Imam. He said, "May all believers identify with the one God and bear witness to true brotherhood." Then the Imam showed Pope Francis, who stood before the Mihrab praying. Then he looked up fervently to heaven. The Imam said, The time has come for us to make love for one another a stronger reality. Indeed, said Phim. I wish to protect your beautiful mosques. What a glorious song they sing!

(Pope Benedict XVI visited the Blue Mosque (30 Nov. 2006) Pope Francis likewise (29 Nov. 2014)

Standing outside, Irma said to Phim, It looks much better from the gallery. We can really see the dome. The spirit's released. It speaks of God (Allah). In our cluttered life, overwhelmed by modern marvels, we forget the miracle these great buildings give. Sal said, Imagine. The first time they entered and looked about in awe. Phim said, It's still amazing, like Hagia Sophia. They went back to the hotel. Irma lent Phim her long skirt. Long sleeved blouse. Green scarf wrapped around. His head bowed down, a strand of beard poking through, Phim climbed up to the gallery.

The guide said, Remember that architect Sinan was ethnically Greek and came from one of the most important regions in Byzantine Christianity — Kayseri in Cappadocia. Highly intelligent, confident and bold. As a Janissary, he became indelibly loyal to the Sultan. What did he feel about his roots? He had the answer already. Konya. He rose to become chief architect. You could say that his whole career was a love poem in stone, inspired by Hagia Sophia, going further. God is God, after all, God is light. See how much light! You can hear him say: I made this for thee.

(Mimar Sinan architect 1489-1588. Süleyman Mosque 1550-1557)

The guide said, The Ottomans under Süleyman the Great were ambitious to be the new Roman Empire, to surpass the Byzantines. Justinian had been a great general and a great builder. His legacy was the Hagia Sophia. Süleyman wanted to show that Islam could do better. This mosque with his name is his statement. Look at those red Egyptian marble columns, taken from Baalbek. That ancient sanctuary was brought here to the true God. Walk around inside. Light! The heavens! Cosmological circles declare the mystery and perfection of God. Sinan has multiplied the number of windows. Light floods the house.

(Süleyman Mosque 1557)

Phim sat on the carpet cross-legged, letting the sun pour through the high windows. A moment of peace. There was so much to look at, and words to read. Phim found a hadith. Abu Huraira reported Allah's Messenger (pbuh) as saying: "He who is given a flower should not reject it, for it is light to carry and pleasant in odour." Then a flowering verse. "By the night as it departs! By the dawn as it brightens! Truly this is the word brought by a most honorable messenger from Allah to Prophet Muhammad." Jibril! The angel so prominent in Luke.

(Sahih Muslim Book 27, Hadith Number 5600. Surat At-Takwir 81.17-19)

Phim looked up into the dome, craning the neck, aah! Stupid vertebrae. Can I lie down on the carpet? Better not. Maybe I should've brought a mirror. The details were wonderful. It'd been brightly restored. White and red stripes in the arches. Yellow in the dome. Wearing a white turban with a red centre, an imam looked at Phim, and started singing the Quran. Phim's eye found a high balustrade in the dome. The voice was so beautiful, lilting, reaching, giving — an angelic voice. He looked at the Quran, "Verily Allah is able to bring him back to life."

(Surat at-Tariq 86.8)

Phim read the guidebook. Sinan had wondered, How shall we ventilate it? All temples lit by oil-lamps or candles were the same. The smoke and soot generated was enormous. Sinan organised a system whereby specific windows would be opened to the prevailing wind. This created a draught which was funneled to a small chimney-chamber. The smoke was carried there and soot deposited. Later used for calligraphic ink. The draught strength was regulated by the apertures. In summer they would keep the mosque cool by similarly noting on which side of the mosque the wind was blowing.

The Imam said, Let me give you a few final hints about this House of God. It was built very quickly, considering its immense size and the quality of the work. Remember how many Christians (and former Christians) still lived in the city and region? Scholars suggest that Süleyman employed a huge army of Muslim and Christian workers. It might have been 50 - 50. Perhaps Jews also. Where's the sanctuary? The prayer hall under the dome. Some people (including myself) think that the name of this complete masterpiece is an important link. What does it say?

Irma said, The mosque and complex were built after the conquest by Mehmed II. Fatih means victory. Yaeli said, Like Cairo, founded by the Arabs. Phim said, Both Christians and Muslims of that age firmly believed that the outcome was decided by God. He gave it to us. Sal said, Have you read the history of this place? Sudan said, The first Mosque didn't survive, unlike the later Sinan triumphs. Joseph stood there silent. Phim waited quietly, and listened. Long ago voices, ancient tongues, future songs mingled together in peace. Irma, an answer is here, and also in Haga Sophia.

(Mehmed II the Conqueror. First Mosque built 1463-1470)

Phim thought again upon the Ottoman granting asylum to the Jews at the time of the Inquisition. A principle being the destruction of another people's holy places brings with it, in one form or another, the whirlwind of destruction. It may take a millennium. Why should that be so? Phim pondered again. Surely it was true for the children of Abraham. House after house came tumbling down. Wasn't Jesus himself a house? Can we step back further and find the holy one and the loving one in the mother or fathers of all life? Wasn't each life a holy house?

The man said, During Ramadan about a million visitors file by to view the holy relics. Muhammad's own mantle, a tuft of beard, in other places, a Quran. Many pilgrims are in tears. There are strong feelings because of a deep connection with the goodness of God, taught by Muhammad, a true father, prophet and guide — the precious feeling that he wore the garment, and that I am able to be close to him who gave so much to my family, my people, and my faith. Islam bonds us together strongly in unity and love. We are such diverse peoples.

(Relic held at Hırka-ı Şerif [Holy Cloak] Mosque [built 1851] Istanbul.)

327   Şehzade Mosque

The guide said, This was Sinan's
apprentice work, but it's an
accomplished jewel. Compare the plan
with the Hagia Sophia. Around the
dome we have four semi-domes, within
a larger square structure. It's beautifully
harmonious. It stands free of the
cluttering buttresses that obscure Hagia
Sophia. Lovely round dome with
half-domes and smaller domes — a
joyful allegory — the One in the centre
surrounded by angels.   Phim said,
There's a renaissance spirit in the work,
seen in the festive color scheme. It
reminds me of Florence.   Irma said, It
could easily be a Russian orthodox
cathedral.

(Shehzade Mosque 1548)

Sudan gazed up at the joyful arches and domes of the Prince's Mosque and thought again about how science was a true revelation of God. For 200 years there'd been an important discovery every decade. Step by step eternal truths had been given; truths that had been hidden from ancient faith. Secrets of far away stars; the electrical currents in the human body. Secular society could be God's way to bring us together. We share hospitals in every city. Same training, same culture. There was good international law. Why do the children of Abraham still persist in the old disunity?

(Shehzade Mosque 1548)

Joseph said, One might think at first, it's an orthodox cathedral, and then one notices that it's a harmonious mosque, with half domes circling the full dome in the centre, a perfect square and circle. Sinan has decided that there will be nothing greater than Hagia Sophia, and God has given Hagia Sophia to Islam, so therefore let us praise God with this beautiful structure, repeated many times. It's as though Rumi were to say, via the medium of hall and dome, one day Heaven will come, and we will be united in praising God who is Love.

(Shehzade Mosque 1548)

It was a public lecture and performance by two virtuoso friends, Japanese and Turkish. They were talking about Mozart and Beethoven. Music has the power to heighten the spirit. Music can lift the mind to a realm of "cognitive heaven." What does that mean, asked Phim. Yaeli said, Music helps you to conceptualize God. The Japanese woman said, The sublime abstraction of music is so pure and chaste. It is passionate for life, filled with compassion for humanity. The Turkish man said, It is truly Allah. The woman said, Yes — remember that pulsing motif? Beethoven! I hear life overcoming death.

(Inspired by the work of Mitsuko Uchida & Fazil Say, fictional event)

The Turkish man said, Let me illustrate our conversation. He sat at the grand piano, and started playing. Hunched over, concentrating, he made curious gestures of giving as he played. Who was he talking to? Phim closed his eyes. It was a prayer. You sing with your fingers. The stars arose and light entered the dark. The pulsing notes are points of light. We can hope in them. We are walking up a stairway. The stars of Orion are stepping stones. Only stars in a cloudless sky. Then the moon arose, a warm golden-yellow climbing to silver-white.

(Fazil Say playing Beethoven Piano Sonata 14 "Moonlight" Adagio)

The tiles are extraordinary, said Sal. The guide explained, The Ottoman golden century (1500-1600) was shown by the tiles. Chinese porcelain served as inspiration. In the early period it was brilliant blue and white. By mid-century they had developed the tomato-red and greens. In 1616 they commissioned 21,000 tiles for the Sultanahmet Mosque (the Blue Mosque). It declined thereafter. It was too expensive. The intriguing point is that it flourished in Iznik. Descendants of Greeks, former Christians, Muslims? Sal said, The effect is undeniably beautiful. Is there a Sufi unity of purpose in the exquisite work?

(Rustem Pasha Mosque 1561. See also the tiles in Shehzade Mausoleum.)

They were attending a public lecture about prehistoric Anatolia. The Professor said, They dated the cranium to 1.2 million years ago. Homo erectus. Early human beings who walked out of Africa, passing through Anatolia, west to Europe, east to Asia. Crossroads of humanity. Sudan said, So where is God then? Sal said, Walking with us. Irma said, Mother and father, their love and care for the children. God is alive in it always. Yaeli said, We must learn that lesson for the whole world. Sudan said, We must learn it for the whole planet, every insect, every tree.

The Professor said, I'm a Turk with mingled ancestry, like millions in this region. Visit the Ancient Orient Museum. All this knowledge was unknown only five generations ago. Look, there's the first writing system. 5,000 years ago. Cuneiform. Sumerians. Who were they? Not Semitic. Followed by the Akkadians (c. 2200 BCE), becoming Babylonians (c. 1800 BCE). They were Semitic. Jews and Arabs are Semitic. Assyrians from Akkadians. Semitic. Hittites (c. 1500 BCE)? From the north? Indo-European. Where does Egypt fit in? Streams of language, faith, and civilization evolved; read, learn, change and grow my children.

(With thanks to Rick Steves' Istanbul by Lale Surmen Aran & Tankut Aran.)

The Professor said, Have you thought about the independent evolution of writing systems? It seems likely that early civilizations evolved their own scripts independently. There were perhaps four: Mesoamerica, Egypt, Sumer (Mesopotamia) and China. This happened at more or less the same time, c. 3500-500 BCE (viewed from the long perspective of the human journey). Now consider the relation between psychology, social change and faith evolution situated in time. Independent developments; interconnected also. There are many common features. The origin is the same, from within developing man. Phim said, Yes, faith must proclaim our family unity.

They stopped at a shop which had a
glass cabinet of thin dried round leaves,
the size of a large hand, painted with
vibrant colours and Arabic calligraphy.
Flowers were used to enfold messages.
I like this, said Phim. A cobalt blue
border containing daisy-like flowers,
with gold edging. Arabic letters danced
in the centre with flakes of brilliant
orange. What does it say?   God is love,
said the artist, an Armenian. These are
my "leaves of understanding and love"
with messages from the great faiths.
Missionary leaves for peace.   Phim said,
How wonderful. I'll take five please.

(Inspired by Nick Merdenyan artist. Grand Bazaar, Istanbul. Gouache on leaves.

Dieffenbachia and caladium leaves.)

A shop selling nazar boncuğu. These were protective amulets to ward off the evil eye. Phim said, What is the evil eye? The shop owner said, It's bad fortune that comes to you when you are fortunate, when someone praises you too much, when there is envy. It's an evil spirit invited by evil intentions. Guard against it by holy words or various ancient traditions. The amulet is one ancient remedy. It's a good eye. Blue, the sky-color, was a holy color almost universally. Sudan said, Those amulets could scare off birds, especially sparrows. Sparrows were unwelcome in ancient Egypt.

(Grand Bazaar, Istanbul. Nazar from Arabic "sight" and boncuğu Turkish for "bead.")

Phim said, I'm going to have a haircut. Saç Sakal please. He sat down and fell asleep. He woke up. The barber took a swab of cotton wool on a stick, soaked it and lit it. Phim watched with alarm. He flicked it into Phim's right ear, and rubbed, and did the same with the left. Phim felt the hot flame. He then applied a small electric razor. Phim's hairy ears were clean shaven. To finish with he pushed his thumbs deep into Phim's shoulders. Grim dungeons crumbled. His mind cleared. Phim actually started to sing, Tralala!

(Grand Bazaar, Istanbul. Saç: Haircut. Sakal: shave)

Phim was playing backgammon in a café. A friendly man with a lugubrious look was teaching some words. We use Persian. One is yek. Two is du. Three is se. The triangles are called kapı (door). Dice are kemik (bones). You kiss your fist and roll, saying "hadi kemik!" (come on bones). Later Phim dreamt he was watching a tournament. On one side were Justinian and Süleyman. The counters were Mosques and Churches. The other moved his pieces, snipping with his mouth. Phim looked at them, demons on fire, searching houses for plunder.

(Grand Bazaar, Istanbul.)

How about a Turkish coffee, said Sudan. It was a small homely cafe. Wooden furniture from thirty years ago. High on the wall a turbaned man sitting on a donkey. The owner, a bald mustachioed friendly character, took the coffee from the gas and poured it out. Thick black fragrant coffee. A cube of lokum. He told them about his family. They'd been in the neighborhood for centuries. Originally they supported the upkeep of Aya Sofiya. This is my daughter. She works part-time. Studying archaeology at the university.   How interesting, said Irma.   She said, There's so much still to discover.

The guide said, Motifs that you see in carpets are also found in Mosque decorations and tiles. Many go back to ancient days. Remember that the Turks came from the Altai mountains. Motifs are talismanic. They are for protection. The cross motif turns away the evil eye. Is this a pre-Christian idea connecting with the later Christian belief? A stylised hands-on-hips figure remembers the ancient mother goddess. Fertility. Human figure for happiness. Motifs for happy marriage. Running water is good. The eye motif is strong. The star motif is holy both from ancient times and in Islam. Six-pointed and eight-pointed.

(Tree of life motif is often used to symbolise life after death & hope of heaven)

It was a modern design with vibrant colors. She said, It's called "Heavenly Flowers." There are seven colors. This is a kirkit. It was a metal tamper. You have to strike the threads in the middle. She bashed the line of threads, packing them tight. Then she ran the scissors along the top, snipping away the excess wool, leaving it tight and smooth.   How do you know which color to tie? asked Irma. It looks so complex.   The weaver said, We have a design-plate which we must follow. Her fingers moved with rapid dexterity, too quick to see.

(Grand Bazaar, Istanbul. Kirkit: carpet comb)

Later, Phim thought about her fingers, tying the knots and jamming them tight, patiently hour after hour, day after day, following the colored diagram, building the carpet, each motif coming to life. Six months? Carpet weaving was hard work. Were they holy people? Ordinary people no doubt, part of a family, a mother or a daughter. Sell the carpet and earn enough food and clothing for half a year. Phim suddenly remembered the thick-piled expensive green and brown carpet his mother had bought when he was a boy. Muddy shoes one afternoon, how angry she'd been.

Loops of wool knotted around two warps standing in the air five millimeters, tightly packed by the wefts. It was all you needed to achieve the firm texture. The pile meant that it would last, compared to a woven rug. Another childhood memory came. They were playing bowls in the park. Phim was watching. Phim slipped his brown sandals off, and walked barefoot on the cool green. He watched the bowls run smoothly curving. He marvelled at the crisscross patterns. Darker and lighter shades of emerald. Daddy, how'd they make the green look so nice?

The guide was enthusing. The central field is a forest of animals. It's as if you're in an amazing landscape, with both real and fantastic creatures. In the borders are several layers of scrolling arabesques. Animal heads are hidden in the foliage. The calligraphy reinforces the visual language, its verdant beauty is evoked: "Come, for the spring breeze has renewed the promise of the meadow." Other lines praise the king calling on him to enjoy eminence forever. In this carpet we see complexity and beauty, with advanced use of silks and dyes. This is assuredly a work of high art.

(Inspired & adapted from text by Met. Museum NY about Safavid "Emperor's Carpet.")

Sal said, Fragments of the holy Kaaba stone are embedded in the walls of the Mosque. This was an important statement. Sinan's saying, God made us the guardians of Mecca, and granted us Istanbul, the Christian sanctuary, to be returned to Him. Now Istanbul and Mecca are one (in spirit, though it's not possible to rival Mecca). I've tried to make this city beautiful for God.   Phim said, It was a pure fiery zeal, God one God!   Irma said, The tiles are very good. The flowers spell the name of God. The Chinese peony is a rose for God.

(Sokollu Mehmed Pasha Mosque, Kadırga, 1571)

The guide said, It's a rectangular
building. Central part octagonal. The
octagon is misaligned. The sides are of
different lengths. The doors are unevenly
placed. Several scholars suggest that the
plans were not followed closely. The
builders had to improvise. They did well,
however. Look at the dome, held up by
eight arches, with supporting pillars.
Sixteen ribs with eight windows. How
pleasing it appears! Elegant Hagia
Sophia prototype. Procopius said: "By
the sheen of its marbles it was more
resplendent than the sun." Verde Antique
serpentine and red Synnada columns,
resting on bases of blue-veined
Proconnesian marble from Marmora.

(Little Hagia Sophia, former Church of Ss Sergius and Bacchus 532-36. With thanks to Robin Pierson.)

The Mosque had been converted from the Myrelaion Church, an ancient convent founded by the Emperor Romanos (c. 950). It was built above a rotunda which became a cistern.   Phim said, Many ancient Churches were built close to reservoirs.   Joseph said, A holy connection.   There was cool white decoration inside the Mosque.   The Imam said, Welcome. Here's a good thought. Both Christian and Muslim are children of the same father. God obviously, but the Jewish faith, which we could signify by Abraham.   Yaeli said, Yes. Why should the children fight one another?   Sal said, The Father loves them both.

(Bodrum Mesipasha Mosque. Myrelaion Monastery "place of myrrh." The rotunda has survived.)

Phim searched for information about the Pertevniyal Valide Sultan Mosque. It got blocked. Articles appeared claiming it was fiction. It galled his spirit. Then, at last, pictures appeared. It was a rococo blend of classic Ottoman features, with influence from contemporary Russian Orthodox Cathedrals. A small jewel. An opulent domestic palace in which to pray. Intriguing to Phim, a blend of styles, tantalizing him with the thought of a heavenly place in which the pious of both sides could be in love with one another. Built in three years? When was that? Following victory in the Crimean war?

(Last major Ottoman Mosque built 1869-71 for the Valide Sultan)

Phim was caught up in a powerful feeling. They were walking on the paving stones, which were ancient graves. There was a flourishing tree. Walking down the stairs into the sanctuary. It had been restored. The air was alive, and he looked for somewhere to be still. Hope and joy together.   Sal, he said, how beautiful the water appears. They had lit it to appear sky-blue turquoise. It gurgled pleasantly. An ancient healing spring had been given by Justinian to Mary, the Blessed Virgin. Sal said, The old word for spring is source, isn't it?

(Monastery of the Mother of God at the Spring, Church of the Life-giving Spirit, restored 1835. Balıklı.)

There was a picture of fish swimming in the marble basin. The Turks had named the place Balıklı (with fish). Irma read from the guidebook.   "According to legend, on the day of the conquest a monk was frying fish in a pan near the source. When they told him about the fall of the city, he said that he'd believe it only if the fish in the pan came back to life. At his words they jumped back into the spring and began swimming." Yaeli said, It rings true, doesn't it. Turkish wisdom?   Joseph said, It sounds like Nasreddin Hodja.

(Sanliurfa Holy Pool [Abraham's pool] is called Balıklı Göl.)

Phim was searching with his iPhone for information in English about the Ottoman Empire which would give a warm generous appraisal. Article after article, book after book, produced the same picture. Hostile accounts. Even the history books written by Turks seemed to be dyed in the same color. Sal, it's a lead coffin-lid — how can we learn to love one another with this on top? I want a more balanced picture. Sal said, It's our task, isn't it. To notice it and try to heave it off.   Sudan said, Understanding information bias is a big step forward.

The guide said, When Mehmed the Conqueror took possession of Constantinople (1453), he intended to make it the flourishing capital of his empire. The Ottomans inherited from earlier Islam the concept of public institutions (imaret) supported by income from attached businesses (vakif). The imaret could be a mosque, madrasa, hospital, traveller's lodge, fountain, road or bridge; the supporting income came from inns, markets, bath houses, shops and mills. The imaret were generally for the public good, and the vakif donated their profits to the upkeep of the imaret. The vakif were servants in perpetuity of the public good.

(Topkapı Palace; Topkapı Sarayı; ṭopḳapə sarāyə; lit. "cannon gate palace.")

Phim said, We saw this kind of thing in Cairo.   The guide said, It was a fundamental principle, developed from the Graeco-Romans, who established a city core-complex, with agora and temples. Under Islam, the vakif were serving God, so they were guaranteed to survive even if the dynasty changed. The charitable endowments (the shops) were overlooked by a Nazir (inspector) to make sure the true purpose was fulfilled. Otherwise, given human nature, the profits would go somewhere else. Sal chuckled, That must have been a difficult job.   The guide said stiffly, The stability and longevity was an Ottoman achievement.

The guide continued, Each city had its own Great Mosque. Mehmed ordered the construction of a bedestan (covered market) as an endowment to support the Great Mosque of Istanbul, the Hagia Sofia. Shops branched out from the centre, lining the alley, forming a guild of similar goods. Roofed with stone, avenues of civility. Mehmed went on to build medreses (institutes of education), a school for children, library, hospital, traveller's hostels, a refectory. Poor could receive food and care. Other hospitals were added, one for women and one for non-Muslims. All the expenses were met out of the charitable endowments.

(Information adapted from Halil Inalcik, *The Ottoman Empire: The Classical Age 1300-1600*. 1994.)

The guide said, Did you not visit the Haseki Sultan Imaret (1552) when you were in Jerusalem? This was a charitable refectory that distributed up to a thousand loaves of bread daily to a wide variety of people. Many were Ottoman employees but 400 were from the wretched poor. These charitable institutions took careful note of whom they were giving to and where they might be coming from. You couldn't just turn up with a sack and walk off with a hundred loaves. Such institutions fulfilled the godly command to be charitable, a central pillar of Islamic identity.

(Founded by Roxelana [Hurrem Sultana] 1504-1558, wife-consort of Suleiman the Great)

Phim found an Ottoman TV saga. In a moment he was engrossed. Alexandra was dancing in front of Suleiman the Magnificent (c. 1520). Daughter of a Ukrainian Orthodox minister, captured in a slave raid, sold into the Harem. Large intelligent eyes. Stunningly beautiful. I will win his heart and rule his mind. Suleiman was bowled over. She converted, changed her name to Hürrem, and ruled. How art can respond to our needs, dressing up the truths, challenging the dullness. The Shakespearean Henriad. Tolstoy. Ottoman glory. Ottoman struggle. How well it was to work it through in art.

(*Magnificent Century* series 1 & 2 2011-2017 199 episodes.)

They were holding demonstrations of Ottoman Cuisine in the Palace Kitchens. Irma looked up at the huge chimneys. It was a large area, taking up a significant percentage of the palace. Phim said, They certainly liked good food! A huge army of cooks and assistants fed the Palace and dependents. The guide said, It worked very smoothly. Products of all kinds were brought it, paid for, prepared and served. If you come with me, we'll teach you some Ottoman cooking. There's a lesson on how to make Ottoman Sherbet, and also chicken with almonds.

The cook said, Sherbet is made with cherries, plums and spices. You can also use grapes.   A kilo of fruit. Half a cup sugar.   One cinnamon stick. Three cloves. A litre of water. Fruit, water and spices in the pan. Boil for thirty minutes. Fruit becomes soft. Transfer to strainer. Add the sugar to the remaining fruit juice. You can vary the amount of sugar or add honey. Add a slice of lemon. Boil for a further five minutes. Strain it and allow to cool. Dilute with water. Serve with ice!

(Sherbet comes Turkish şerbet, from Arabic šarba drink.)

The cook said, Mahmudiye with honey is classic Ottoman cuisine, with its sweet, sour and spicy taste. It was served to guests in the Topkapı Palace at the feast of Princes Şehzade Cihangir and Bayezid, sons of Suleiman the Magnificent (1539). You'll need half a boiled chicken, chopped into cubes, 2 tablespons butter, 3-4 tablespoons olive oil, 1 onion, 3 tablespoons almonds, 3 tablespoons raisins, 5-6 dried apricots, half a teaspoon: salt, black pepper, cinnamon; 2 tablespoons honey, half a lemon, serve with orzo pilaf rice. Saute chopped onion in butter, add olive oil, almonds, chicken, fruit and the rest.

(Mahmudiye comes from Arabic Mahmud meaning praise or praiseworthy.)

361 Keşkül

The cook said, Keşkül was the wandering dervish's begging bowl. Money collected in the bowl would be used to feed the poor. Milk pudding was often served in the same kind of bowls. Hence the name of the dish, transferred from the bowl. 1 litre of milk, 150 gr. sugar, half a cup ground almonds, 1 teaspoon vanilla extract, half a cup corn starch, 200 ml milk, 1 egg. Gently roast the almond powder. Heat milk. Mix 200 ml milk, cornstarch and egg, whisk until smooth, add to hot milk, add ingredients, allow to cool. Bowl of sweet white pudding.

(Keşkül Milk Pudding, Ottoman charity.)

A fantasy fled through Phim's mind. Imagine trying to steal it. A turbaned statue of the Sultan. The diamond encrusted dagger in his belt. Emeralds like greengages. Sudan, have you got my legs. Phim wore a headlight. Special glass clamps. Heave up the glass case. Easy does it. Pull out the dagger. Aah, nearly dropped it. Swinging wildly. Fumbled. Placed the fake one. Lower the case. Haul me up, Sal. All clear. Imbecile, said Yaeli, you've put the wrong one back. Alarm bells ring. Guards appear with pistols. Phim and crew are in the sky-light. Look, they're up there!

(Inspired by *Topkapi* (1964) film. Gilles Ségal "Giulio - the Human Fly.")

Phim wondered about the dagger. Made for the Shah of Persia (1747). He was assassinated, so the Sultan kept it. He'd known? Made it as a warning? Three massive emeralds on the hilt. Green for God. A watch at the end, a jeweled octagonal lid. A dagger to tell the time. Time's up, Shah. Time to meet God. Or maybe it signified the holy word. Gold set with diamonds. Enamelled bowl of fruit. Emerald at the sheath-tip. I wonder how sharp it was. Sal said, It looks like a kukri. Sudan said, It pulls on deep-rooted instinct, doesn't it.

(Watch made by George Clarke, London, clock-maker to the Ottomans 1725-1766.)

They feasted their eyes on the sumptuous jewels. The spoonmaker's diamond. An egg-shaped monster adorned with a double row of diamonds. The lighting danced and sparkled. A blue flame flickered within. Phim wondered about the display, remembering a Russian Icon of Mary with a glittering jeweled cover. To honor and show how precious she is. They didn't use jeweled ornamentation in the mosques. Sal, what does Islam say about jewels? Worldly beauty, said Sal. You could dress a princess in diamonds but her soul should be bright as a star. The Sultan's aigrette should show his love for God.

(Aigrette: jewel with feather adorning the imperial turban)

Phim said, Why did the Ottomans prize porcelain so highly?   They were looking at the Topkapı collection, second only to China.   The guide sniffed in disdain. Because it is very beautiful. Think what was used for tableware c. 1250 CE. The English ate off wooden boards. In Italy, earthenware plates. The Seljuks began buying porcelain. They would have known about it for centuries. Tableware of exquisite quality, fit for a Khan. Now we are Khan (Sultan), we'll buy the best. It was translucent, lightweight, very strong and you could glaze it with beautiful pictures. We'll be like the Sons of Heaven.

The guide looked down his large nose at Phim. Nobody but the Chinese knew how to make it. It was like silk. The Turks thought that food on such plates would be protected. Celadon ware had this reputation. We'll use porcelain tiles in the mosques and praise God. Cobalt supplied the blue. The Chinese artisans were highly refined. Look at this. Ming finches depicted with delicate detail, perched in a blossoming tree. Simply but beautifully done with shades of blue and white. The leaves appear to move in the breeze. Pearly white background. How refined it is.

Yaeli said, What an elegant space. The golden taps emerged from sober grey-veined marble. There were high-domed ceilings with small round windows, called elephant's eyes, arranged in a beautiful pattern. The guide said, The Ottomans inherited from the Romans a love of hot water and created a culture of cleanliness that remains today. They had indoor plumbing long before the European palaces. Yaeli said, Islam shared with the Jews the love of fresh water. Delight in water — God's gift of being free from sin. Phim said, How good it is to wash yourself before you enter the House of God.

Breathtaking, said Phim.   Sal said, If we enter into the spirit of the decoration, every inch is praising God.   Sudan said, Fireplace with cone, like a soldier's helmet, holy fire of faith.   Irma said, The panel of mother-of-pearl inlay is good. Surely it symbolizes the holy scripture.   Joseph said, The ten petaled rose must signify God.   Phim said, It was a throne room. There's the golden throne.   Sal said, They held national council meetings. It would be a glorious Ottoman allegory. By Allah, we shall make a world of peaceful trade. All peoples — be happy and prosper under God.

(Baghdad Kiosk 1639 in honor of Sultan Murad IV's Baghdad Campaign)

Sudan said, A lesson from the good tulip. It was found in the rugged Pamirs by nomadic Turkic tribes. The Seljuks brought it to Konya. It appeared on tiles. Highly valued from early times, a beautiful herald of spring-life returning; the Persian name Lale was written with the same letters as Allah. It had talismanic power. It was put on armour for protection. Later, it was cultivated by the Dutch. A mad speculative fever for red and white varieties developed. Later, Ahmed imported Dutch varieties. It became a symbol of Ottoman decadence. He cares more for flowers than his people!

(Sultan Ahmed III ruled 1703–1730)

They'd restored the walls, and stripped
back the plaster, to leave the building
standing unadorned. In the apse there
was a semi-circle, for choir or council.
Above this were three plain glass
windows. The natural light poured in.
Joseph said, Remember that they met
here for important talks. How well
they've allowed the Spirit to fill this
place. Let's stand in prayer. Our love for
God can turn the world to peace.   Phim
said, I'd like to hear a choir fill this place
with holy song — choirs of the
Abrahamic family.   Yaeli said, A peace
concert: Jew, Christian and Muslim.

(Ancient Church c. 330, built & rebuilt. Site of important Church Council 381.)

The guide said, What is Islamic Art? It's a category invented at the Louvre a hundred years ago. There's such diversity throughout the nations and cultures that profess Islam. But perhaps there is one theme. Essentially, Islamic culture is pious and devotional. Art (in the West) is the human image. For Islam (following the Jews) that image is pagan. Therefore the art is calligraphic and symbolic. It is geometrical and floral. God is the theme. How many ways can we say His name? To love this art you must love God. You must become partly Muslim. Yes, said Phim.

(Turkish Islamic Arts Museum)

Look, said Yaeli, they're comparing two carpets, one's a Muslim prayer carpet for prostration, the other's a parochet for the Torah Ark. The Muslim one has a lamp with a flame hanging in the centre of a triple arch; the Jewish one has a lamp inscribed with the Holy Name (Hebrew). Jewish artisans fled Spain (1492) and came to Istanbul. The Jewish carpet has an inscription which says it is a gate for the Lord. The lamps are a symbol of God, hanging in a niche, the Holy Word, the Torah, a mihrab. It could be a window on paradise.

(Ottoman Prayer Carpet 1575-90; Ottoman Torah Ark curtain 1608. Turkish Islamic Arts Museum. Inspired by Smarthistory clip.)

Phim said, That's Thutmose III's column. Egypt's greatest imperial conqueror. War and conquest in the region until Ataturk's noble republic (1923).   Yaeli said, Egyptian armies and colonies played an important role in the story of Israel.   Joseph said, A lot of blood was spilt here. The terrible Nika Riots (532). I hope they exaggerated the numbers.   Irma said, How did they manage to transport those glorious horses? Were they seeing that it would fall? Let's help ourselves?   Sal said, Always remember, they allowed coexistence. Churches survived.   Phim said, I still think integrated friendly coexistence must be true faith.

(Thutmose III reigned c. 1479-1425 BCE)

Let's do that again, said Phim.   Are you crazy, said Sal.   Joseph said, OK, We'll circle round and go through on the other deck. It was a double-decker tunnel, with traffic coming and going on the two decks. Nothing to see except strips of LED. Traffic signs. Five minutes and they were through.   Yaeli said, Let's speak a word of strength as we go. Irma said, Phim, say something. Sudan said, Too many damn cars. Phim said, Joy to the Greeks and Turks! Yaeli said, Birnānā! Joseph said, En Agalliasei!   Sal said, "Rejoice (Falyafrahū!) in Allah's grace and mercy!"

(Avrasya Tunnel 2016. LXX Ps 100.2 & Quran Jonah 10.58 Falyafrahū let them rejoice!)

They stood on the wharf in Üsküdar looking at the sunset. The sky was darkening as the sun rested on the horizon, very large and golden. To the left was the old city, the minarets like pencils. To the right of the tower was the entrance to the Golden Horn. Like Egypt, it had been a horn of plenty. The Bosphorus had a dark blue metallic sheen. Sudan said, See the sun move. Wonderful, said Yaeli. The tower was in silhouette, small flag held up. Phim said, Is that a star? It became brighter as the sun went down.

(Maiden's Tower, Üsküdar, Asian Istanbul)

The guide said, This garden zone was part of a patchwork of farms within the city confines for feeding the inhabitants. The Ottoman state employed people to farm. Produce was sent to the palace. There was a fight a few years ago to develop the area but the locals banded together and saved it. It's a precious green space. There were allotments growing vegetables and unpaved paths. Sudan said, Why don't they go one further, and make it a nature garden for the future? Are they planting trees and flowers? Why have those guys put a stupid shed over there?

(Aboretum, Üsküdar. Green urban oasis.)

Phim said, How absolutely astonishing. It's an underground temple flooded by holy water. Rows and rows of classical columns held up the roof. A forest of columns. 12 rows of 28, each 5 m apart (a year of columns). It was designed to be a reservoir, filled by the Valens aqueduct. There was a huge Gorgon head turned upside down. The old powers were reversed.   Irma said, It's a mystical city baptism, close to the Hagia Sophia. They stood on the walkway. The columns were lit up. The effect was beautiful. There were fish swimming in the shallow water.

(Built in the 6th century during the reign of Emperor Justinian I)

As they ascended the minaret (by special permission), Phim said to Sudan, It's narrow. The stairs curved round, climbing steeply in the dark. Obviously there'd be no one coming in the other direction. Sal said, These minarets are an Ottoman glory. They bound the stone with cast iron clamps, finishing with intricate detail, and the beauty of the cantilevered balcony. We are columns wearing lovely hats! Allah be thanked for Aya Sofia; we will stand about in eternal praise. Phim clung to the balcony, looking down on the roof. It was fearfully high. Joseph said, God bless this holy city!

As they waited to enter Hagia Sophia, a pale figure with large eyes moved up to Phim and spoke softly, Grief at losing our home Phim, remember these past ages and how the families were swept away, so many exiles and executions. Lonely isolation. Raised to one expectation, condemned to another, how hard it was! In holy sacrifice must we serve. Old friends and opponents meet in the light. Phim said, Who are you? An Osmanoğlu daughter. God bless Turkey and all her people, amen. She faded. Her gentle voice left God in the air. Allah!

The guide explained, When Mehmed II entered the city, the first building he wanted to see was the Hagia Sophia. He was 21 years old. The cathedral was filled with trembling people praying. He ordered that none be harmed and that the church be respected. Then he said, We'll pray here on Friday. It was Tuesday. They arranged for a wooden minaret, mihrab. Christian contents were removed. So it became the number one Imperial Mosque. The name Holy Wisdom was kept. Look, there in large letters, the name of God. Tell me, said the guide, who really made this place?

(Conquest of Constantinople 1453)

381   Square the Circle

The guide said, It is remarkable. It's said to have been completed in 5 years 10 months 4 days. Symbolic numbers? With 10,000 workers. Anthemius built four massive columns. A square. On top of them four arches. He filled the spaces between the arches with masonry, creating triangular pendentives. This section was curved to form a circle, the base of the dome. From this he raised forty ribs to the centre. Forty windows set around the base. The dome floats above them. The wooden scaffolding must've been astonishing. A small forest of timber must have supported the work.

(Hagia Sophia built by Justinian in 532-37).

They were looking at a replica of the
Holy Crown. It was made in
Constantinople (c. 1070). It resembled
the Byzantine diadem, seen in the
Hagia Sophia mosaic of John II
Comnenus. Pure gold, with a line of
pearls above and below. Look, said Irma,
at the enamel of Christ on his heavenly
throne. Trees from the Garden of
Paradise left and right. Like flames. A
large blue sapphire under Christ. The
archangels faced one another, with blue
and black feathers and green haloes. It
had pendilia with bright garnets.
Three-petalled flowers or three-eyed
stars - holy guards of the king.

(Holy Crown of Hungary presented by Emperor Michael VII Doukas to King Géza I.)

There was another replica. It was an exact copy of an ivory angel held in the British Museum, on display in the Narthex. Phim gasped at the workmanship. Sculpted from an elephant's tusk, it was the right-panel of a diptych, dating from 525-550. An angel stood at the top of the stairs, holding an orb and cross in his right hand, and a staff in his left. Large-eyed, curly-haired, feminine. The details were very fine. The acanthus on the columns. Rosettes. Look, said Phim, at Gabriel on the Cathedral walls. He held a crystal orb. Is it the same angel?

(Byzantine Ivory Angel, British Museum. Byzantine artifacts imagined as if on display in the Narthex.)

Phim remembered La Giralda which had similar ramps. There were seven, leading up to the north gallery, where the Byzantine noblewomen would attend the service.   The guide said, This is where the Empress stood. They looked down the whole length of the cathedral. Up above there was the beautiful round calligraphy of Allah, on the right, and Muhammad on the left. In the apse, there was Mary enthroned with the Christ child. The Mihrab looked south-east.   Irma said, I feel holiness in these signs standing in peace.   Phim said, It's meant to be. A question and an answer.

(La Giralda, minaret of the Great Mosque, now the bell tower of Seville Cathedral.)

385   Marbles

Phim said, The first appearance of the Cathedral was truly glorious. The lower walls were clad in slabs of expensive marble, cut into panels to display mirror images of strange angelic forms, with different colours and tones. The upper half was clad in gold tesserae, small glass mosaics with gold leaf. Crosses were the only decoration. No icons. Look at that! A picture made with inlaid marble. The temple curtains are drawn. Holy cross stands victor upon four steps. Pendilia hang down as from a crown. Holy priest Christ the king. Two doves above. Note the acanthus — our flourishing faith.

(Possibly a symbolic picture of the Hagia Sophia. Four steps are the Gospels?)

A young man ran quickly around inside the nave, turning back and squealing as he looked towards his mother. What's he doing, thought Phim, with annoyance. His mother ran up and took his arm and said something to quieten him. He subsided, appearing pleased. Phim realized that there was something going on inside his head. It was excitement and joy in the space of Hagia Sophia, overflowing in this spontaneous response. Who cares about manners or conventions when God's before me? Let me run round in circles forever in joy. A sudden thought flickered, shall I do the same?

Irma said, The fiery seraphim with swirling feathers. The guide said, The seraphim were painted on the pendentives during nineteenth century restoration. There were mosaic icons earlier. Sudan said, How strange that the fearful dinosaurs should survive to be such a beautiful form. Phim said, The original seraphim are fearful. Sal said, How much we can see here. The wings of the First Nations; the flames of the sun. Yaeli said, There's a Japanese story about wearing feather robes. Joseph said, We have a prophetic description. Read or listen. It's worth thinking about. Would Isaiah have drawn a picture?

(Is. 6:2-6. Cp Seraph on the walls of the Jerusalem International YMCA.)

Irma said, Look at the way she floats above the windows. She really is above the sky.   Joseph said, She holds on her lap the golden Christ Child. It recalls her pregnancy and her life, which encompasses the life of Jesus.   Phim said, She's a holy mandorla presenting Christ.   Yaeli said, In her most exalted nature she's offering the divine gift, who himself has so much meaning and truth. Joseph said, The Holy Mother looks upon the altar from the place of highest honor. Did we understand? In the walls and the dome I am here, and Christ within.

(With thanks to Steven Zucker (quote) and Beth Harris, Smarthistory, Khan Academy.)

389   Deësis

Warm loving gaze. The hand blesses. His hair flows. His right eye looks straight at you and his left eye looks away to the left — how many times did we betray him? Phim thought about this. Immediately his mind returned to the earliest memory. Mother and father and all things — Jesus. I didn't say I love you to her when I could have done. She needed to hear it. I know it now. A regret unhealable. I love you Mum. I'll say it to my friends, Joseph, Sal, Sudan, Yaeli, Irma. It helped. May God carry my love to her.

(The Deësis mosaic, Δέησις, "Entreaty," probably dates from 1261.)

Phim said, After all is said and done, after all the badness, what remains? A wonder we can share; a place to hope for God. We can turn ourselves away to Him; what shall we know Him to be? Irma said, Don't say badness, Phim. Yaeli said, We must know the cost to know the love.   Sal said, We must finish with love but we simply have not learned enough.   Sudan said, Correct! Time hastens on. How healthy are the Bosphorus waters? What about the beauty of our world?   Joseph said, We can pray together, in peace, in love.

Well-built, fair complexion, blue-eyed, thin-faced, eyes rolling, cheeks drawn in anguish. He ran over quickly, grabbed Phim and rushed out. He tied him up. He proceeded to haul him up onto the roof, muttering insanely. Snatches of Arabic, Turkish and Greek. Grunting like an ape and cackling like a chicken. He had unearthly strength.   Let me go, said Phim.   The man laughed madly. What do you want, asked Phim.   I am Homo sophiens, he said, and bellowed, Gaalaahaad! Shall I cut your throat my BaaBaa! Come here, let me stroke it open.

The lunatic held Phim at the edge, on the point of either hurling him down or cutting his throat. He issued demands. I will release the BaaBaa if you promise to stop piddling on the wall behind Waterloo Station. It offends the laws of God. It appeared he was English. Phim tried conversation. From London? I was. Like cricket? Slow bowler, googlies. Wicket-keeper. Phim's hazy knowledge told him something was wrong. Bowled in pads. Nice and slow. Didn't need me coz I bowled 'em. How about letting me go? We're all going to deeeeee! he shrieked, sounding Scottish.

393   Bad

The Turkish Police were talking to Sal.
Yaeli said, Fly a drone with a speaker.
Pipe him some music.   One of the
Turks said, Why not try Michael
Jackson? We found it worked a treat
once.   The drone rose slowly, bathing
the dome with "Bad" from the Bad
Album.   Through   binoculars   they
watched the madman twitching, his face
grimacing with pain, possessed with the
will to dance.   Noooo, he screamed,
you throw angels at me. You cheat again.
They   turned   up   the   volume.   The
pigeons   fled.   Stop, he yelled, and
started to climb down, leaving Phim
clinging on desperately.

(Michael Jackson (1958-2009), songwriter and performer, "Bad." 1987)

Profile

Stean Anthony

I'm British, based in Japan. I've written a series of books of poetry promoting understanding and peace. Find out more from the list at the end of this book. I have also published *Eco-Friendly Japan*, Eihosha, Tokyo (2008). *Monday Songs 1-7,* and *Eitanka 1* (pdf file textbook freely available on website – and sound files). Thanks to Yamaguchi for kind help.

New Projects
Maiko (verses on the theme of Japanese Dance)
Saint Mark 450 (Japanese translation of the Gospel)
Hagios Paulos 4 (verses on the theme of Saint Paul)
Japan Angels 2 (little verses)
Story of Phim (cont. vol 6 Greece, vol 7 Italy vol 8 Japan)

Author's profits from this publication to be divided equally between the following institutions. The principal Jewish Synagogue (United Synagogue and Bevis Marks) and Muslim Mosque in London (London Central Mosque and East London Mosque), the Patriarchal Stavropegic Monastery of St John the Baptist in Tolleshunt Knights, the Coptic Christian Center in Stevenage, and the National Shrine of Our Lady of Walsingham, Norfolk, England.

Stean Anthony Books with Yamaguchi Shoten. Original poetry & translations & adaptations. Most are textbooks.

- *Selections from Shakespeare 1-5* (selected passages)
- *Great China 1-4* (transl. of classical Chinese poetry)
- *Kŏngzĭ 136* (poems based on the sayings of Confucius)
- *Manyōshū 365* (transl. of ancient Japanese poems)
- *One Hundred Poems* (poems based on the Japanese classical anthology 百人一首 *Hyakunin Isshu*)
- *Heiankyō 1* (translations of ancient Japanese poems)
- *Inorijuzu* (Buddhist & Christian words for peace)
- *Soulsongs* (poems for peace in Jerusalem)
- *Sufisongs* (poems for peace in Jerusalem)
- *Pashsongs* (songs & poems by Stean Anthony)
- *Bird* (poems on the theme of birds)
- *Sport* (poems on the theme of sport)
- *Hana 1* (poems on the theme of flowers)
- *Japan Angels 1* (little poems on the theme of angels)
- *Tsukinowaguma no Ko* (on moon bears & ecology)

- *Songs 365* (poems based on the Psalms)
- *Songs 365* (in Japanese poems based on the Psalms)
- *Songs for Islam* (poems based on verses in the Quran)
- *Isaiah Isaiah Bright Voice* (poems inspired by *Isaiah*)
- *Saint Paul 200* (poetic phrases from St Paul)

416

- *Hagios Paulos 1-3* (poetry based on the life of St Paul)
- *Gospel 365* (based on the Synoptic Gospels)
- *Saint John 550* (poetic version of *St John*)
- *Saint John 391* (verses in Japanese from the Gospel)
- *Saint John 190* (verses Japanese from Catholic Letters)
- *Saint Matthew 331* (songs Japanese from the Gospel)
- *Saint Mary 100* (poems dedicated to St Mary)
- *Saint Mary 365 Book 1-8* (calendar of poems themes relating to Mary, flowers, icons, prayers, scripture)
- *Saint Luke 132* (verses in Japanese from the Gospel)
- *Saint Mark 454* (verses in Japanese - forthcoming)

- *Messages to My Mother 1-7* (essays on faith etc)
- *Mozzicone 1-2* (essays on faith etc)
- *Monday Songs 1-7* (pdf textbooks of English songs)
- *Eitanka 1* (pdf textbook teaching poetry)
- *Psalms in English* (80 lectures in English teaching the Psalms pdf textbook)

- *Exnihil* (Book 1 in Phim's story)
- *Bərešitbara* (Book 2 in Phim's story)
- *Enarchae* (Book 3 in Phim's story)
- *Samawatiwal'ard* (Book 4 in Phim's story)
- *Tanrı Dedi Işık Olsun* (Book 5 in Phim's story)

TANRI DEDI IŞIK OLSUN
by Stean Anthony

Company : Yamaguchi Shoten
Address : 4-2 Kamihate-cho, Kitashirakawa
　　　　　 Sakyo-ku, Kyoto, 606-8252
　　　　　 Japan
Tel. 075-781-6121
Fax. 075-705-2003

TANRI DEDI IŞIK OLSUN 定価 2,000円(本体1,818円＋税)

2024年4月20日　初　版

　　　　　　著　者　Stean　Anthony
　　　　　発行者　山 口 ケ イ コ
　　　　　印刷所　大村印刷株式会社
　　　　　発行所　株式会社　山口書店
〒606-8252京都市左京区北白川上終町4-2
　　TEL：075-781-6121　FAX：075-705-2003

ISBN 978-4-8411-0950-4　C1182